Best
Vegan
Science Fiction
& Fantasy

2020

Best
Vegan
Science Fiction
& Fantasy

2020

edited by
B. Morris Allen

IISBN: 978-1-64076-007-3 (e-book)
ISBN: 978-1-64076-008-0 (paperback)

plant
based
press

from
Metaphorosis Publishing

Neskowin

Contents

From the Editor

If there's a silver lining to 2020, with all its COVID-19 problems, it's that — in some countries, for some people — we got to spend more time with our companion animals, and that so many people adopted animals that in some places there were more would-be adopters than animals needing homes. I'd like to hope that all those animals found happy homes, and that with more people introduce to the joys of animal companions, things will improve for animals across the board.

Certainly, there's been a lot of progress on the vegan front, even just during the five years of these anthologies. There are more vegan food and clothing options than ever before. The world — even the United States — is finally getting serious about climate change and even beginning to consider that adopting a vegan lifestyle is one of the key changes we could all make to avoid disaster. It's an idea still on the fringes of the conversation, despite its well-documented benefits, but it *is* part of the conversation. Maybe there's hope that livestock operations will someday be a part of our dismal past that we prefer not to remember. Maybe cities and universities will tear down statues and rename buildings because the honoree was, after all, a meat eater, or, worse, a factory farmer.

In the darker reality of the here and now, we still have a long way to go, but I do think there's light on the horizon. The stories in this anthology, are, on the whole hopeful. While, in keeping with the theme of the *Best Vegan SFF* series, they're not *about* veganism, they are vegan-friendly, and more likely to hold up in the long term than some of their contemporaries.

We're nearing the end of COVID-19, too. As I write this, vaccines are more and more available, with some countries having vaccinated significant proportions of their populations, and others catching up. Let's hope the year continues to improve. Read these stories, and yours will!

B. Morris Allen
Editor
1 May 2021

Lingua Franca

Amelia Fisher

I knew the children had no names, though I didn't understand it. Far had tried to explain it to me, but this was one barrier our strides in communication could not quite breach. She would always be of the city, and I an interloper. In the park, sitting on either side of the silent boy, you could have told that just from looking at us: Far in her machine-tailored suit jacket, me in my worn jeans and patchy self-applied buzz cut. Only one of us fully human, or so I'd been taught.

From the emotions flickering over their faces, I assumed she and the boy were engaged in silent conversation—or whatever the casters called it, since they insisted there were no words. I wasn't sure how letting the boy pick a name he'd never use was supposed to help with his tutoring lessons, but Far had insisted—said it would give the kid something to brag about to his friends. Personally, I doubted any of our pupils ever spoke a word outside of our sessions. Still, I figured there were things she wasn't telling me, or was unable to tell me as a result of what she would sardonically call my 'impairment'. But I'd learned when to stop asking questions long before I set foot in the city itself.

Far sat at the boy's side, leaning over his shoulder to scan the list of names with a kind, flavorless smile.

The thermal regulators set at intervals along the grass softened the spring chill, warping the air around them with distortions of heat. The book propped up on the boy's grass-stained knees was made with real paper, a relic Far must have tracked down from some obscure online dealer. When I first came to the city, I probably would have taken offense at the laziness of that stereotype; it wasn't as if my sort hated technology. I said nothing. I'd been here long enough to know how these things went.

"Pine," Far said aloud. I'd gotten so used to the silence that the sound of a human voice was uncanny. "You like that name?" She met my eyes as she spoke. She always did, as if seeking out my approval, my appraisal of her accent, or maybe because really I was the one she was speaking to. The boy did not look up.

After that Far gave up on speaking in a way that I could perceive. I could hear the chirping of birds, the distant whisper of traffic drifting through the city's floating thoroughfares. Down the hill, children were tumbling over the playground like seed pods caught in a wind flurry, running pell-mell over the grass, hauling themselves up by their skinny arms and swinging back and forth on the hovering metal bars which always dipped lower before their strength gave out. Not one of them spoke, though at intervals they laughed at something I could not hear. They moved like images on a screen, detached from sound. From the dog park down the hill, a single low bark seemed to ride up to us on a vast wave of silence. Even the animals were quiet, well-trained. I kept quiet too.

"Well, that settles it," Far said at last. "Do you want to tell Vaun your name?"

At long last the boy looked up and met my eyes. "Kite," he said. His accent was much stronger than Far's, and the word sounded garbled on his unpracticed tongue. I'd learned to stop correcting him. That was Far's job. My job was to be a novelty and a prop.

"That's a nice name," I said. "What made you pick it?"

"The book had a picture."

"Like the bird, or the toy?"

The boy stared at me blankly for a long time before turning back to his teacher. In my pocket, my handheld buzzed an anxious tattoo of notifications. Probably the family group chat; the thought, sudden and cold, that it might be Nan gave me pause. Maybe my strange companions wouldn't mind if I pulled out my handheld in the middle of a session. They lived in a sea of notifications, after all; other people's thoughts and intentions were the air they breathed. Still, I had some sense of professional decorum. I ignored it for the time being.

Far waited patiently for a moment before saying; "Aloud, please. It's important to practice."

The boy—Kite, now, I supposed—did not sigh, but the conversation expected it. "How can one word mean more than one thing?"

Always so strange, to hear them vocalize. The words were correct enough, but something was missing in the speech itself, a lack of understanding or practice. She watched the boy, her expression unchanged. I noted her professionalism even if I didn't admire it. "It's rude not to include someone in the conversation."

"Not my fault she can't hear us." The more petulant he grew, the more natural his speech sounded. He looked at me then, full of that total stillness I could never convince myself wasn't hiding something else beneath. I met his gaze, trying not to make it a challenge, failing. Casters had no taboos against extended eye contact, and so we inspected each other for much longer than I could be comfortable with. I found myself studying his left eye for a glint of the thing behind it.

When he spoke at last, his expression did not change. "I'm sorry I was rude. I want to keep learning how to speak."

I wondered whether Far was feeding him the right words to say. Even that might be more effort than I should expect from her. "That's okay. Learning a language can be frustrating."

The boy's emotions moved over his face like storm clouds: doubt, irritation, boredom. But he still nodded—stiff, formal—and said, "Especially now that there's only one."

I blinked. "Well, there are quite a few spoken languages. We're speaking English right now, but many people speak Spanish, Chinese—"

His face did not change, but I heard Far sigh again. "No, you will only need to learn a single language to satisfy your extra-curricular requirement. Now, let's move on to the vocal warmups."

After the boy had been sent on his way, picked up by a sleek black car that lifted away from the park and into the transit loop above, Far and I settled at one of the park's many benches. She did this with the metal barrel of a cig between her lips, unlit as of yet, but placed there as soon as there was no chance of the boy or his chaperone seeing it. Her lips curled more easily around it than they did around her professional smile.

"Those aren't real names, you know. They're just words," I said, hating this urge to fill the silence and yet unable to resist it.

"Your 'real' names are just words."

"Old words."

"Oh, well that's alright, then." Far took a drag from her cig. "Let the kid have something to tell his parents."

Skirting the edge of a familiar argument, I decided to retreat. "How'd you pick your name?"

"Opened the dictionary and put my finger down at random." I doubted that. She'd probably done it a few times, until she found one she liked. *The state of being distant.* Words and sound still meant something, no matter what the casters liked to pretend.

In the lull of conversation, I slid my handheld from my pocket. Tocsin's name blinked up at me, but I caught Far staring at me and quickly put it away. She had whisked aside the benevolent placidity of her teaching facade as soon as the cig touched her lips. Now she just looked tired. The park was utterly silent but for the faint hum of the thermal regulators and the distant rumble of cars, the running footsteps of the voiceless children.

The tip of Far's cig flared green as she contemplated me. She might have spoken my language, but the way she looked at me was common to every caster I'd met—all overt, unfiltered feeling. No point keeping emotion off your face when everyone around you could skim it off the top of your biodigital cloud. A world without privacy, and thus without shame. Though sometimes Far's expressions were tinted by a more subtle quirk of her lips or eyebrow, or a sly look I couldn't quite read: expressions of a hidden interiority I liked to think she'd picked up from me. I sometimes wondered if she sent thoughts my way on impulse, a sleet of hellos and goodbyes and questions and jokes that slid off me without my knowledge.

It was that kind of thinking that made me doubt my choice sometimes, the thought of all those words and feelings falling mutely around me in a void I couldn't even feel. But then I'd remember what Nan always said: that the soul wasn't meant to be passed around like a cup of moonshine. How could there be trust without secrets?

Her arm over the back of the park bench shifted to where it didn't quite touch my back, but might have if I leaned back just a little. Again my handheld buzzed against my leg, but if I took it out now, Far would assume I was brushing her off. And, well, I had my own expectations about how this afternoon was going to end.

"How long before you have to go back?"

Before answering, I leaned over to pluck the cig from her lips and raise it to my own, breathing in the taste of— "*Soap?*" I said, making a face as I handed it back.

Far grinned. "Cilantro. New flavor."

"I can see why no one thought of it before." But then I leaned back against the softness of her coat sleeve resting on the back of the bench and said, "Long enough."

After we were done, I peeled my cheek from the rise and fall of Far's rib cage with a sound like pulling off a piece of tape. The temperature modulator hummed busily from the ceiling, dumping a waterfall of chilly air into the otherwise stuffy room, turning my bare skin clammy. Far said nothing as I unspooled myself towards the other side of the bed where the glass of water always sat. Far watched me; I didn't need augmented mental senses to feel her eyes on the curve of my spine.

It had started with an argument about Borges, one of his collections Far was 'muchly surprised' I hadn't read. I'd taken issue with her tone and openly doubted that she owned a copy. By the time we got back to her place, I'd forgotten it entirely. I probably shouldn't have let things continue, but I was never very smart about that sort of thing. Far was available, attractive, and not from the compound, which made things both simpler and more complicated in a way that excited me. And it was a little cute, the way Far spoke; the ornate synonyms and slurring pronunciation, the accent of one who still tasted the words like they were new.

When I looked back, she had tucked one arm behind the back of her head, displaying a dark tuft of hair trimmed to a fashionable length. I couldn't imagine Far doing anything that wasn't fashionable. Her eyes were soft as a piece of fruit that you wouldn't want to eat. She opened her mouth and I braced myself for some brutal insight brought on by the candor of the afterglow.

But what she actually said was, "Can I have some of that water?"

I tipped my head back and drained the glass while holding her eye.

Far sighed. "You're a dick. Is that the right word here? Or would asshole be more appropriate?"

I got up to refill the glass from the nodule on the wall, cool water chilling the glass cupped in my fingers. When I brought it back to her and settled it on the soft dampness of Far's stomach, she sucked in a sharp, relishing breath.

"Neither," I said. "I'm very considerate."

"Hm. You have your moments."

The bob of her throat as she swallowed seemed to move inside of me, too. But what sank into the pit of my stomach wasn't an echo of the unspoken vows we'd been mouthing into each other's bodies for the past hour and a half. Only then I remembered my handheld's frequent buzzing. I fumbled it off the bedside table and was greeted with a storm of notifications. I swiped through them quickly, sliding them across the cool glass like oil over water, and all of them from Tocsin.

Home soon?
Hey dickhead I need to talk to you about smthn
turn your handle on or I'll tell Nan about your porn
For real, where are you?
Vaun, I'm serious.
Let me know when youll be back...
Vauneant?
it's important
hello???

And then, two hours later: *everything's fine but please come talk to me when you can and please don't ask anyone else about me.*

"Shit," I said aloud.

Far shifted against the covers. "Something wrong?"

Thirty-two messages total. If something truly dire had gone down, I'd have heard from more people—I'd have heard from Nan. Tocsin was more brother than cousin to me, but he was also an impulsive little shit, and always dealing with one self-manufactured personal crisis or another. It was probably about a girl, or a wrecked car. Probably nothing at all.

"Not sure," I said, sitting back down on the bed. "I should probably go."

Far turned to look at me. The way she used her eyes sometimes, it made me understand what casting was. "You know, maybe you wouldn't have to run around so much if you were making enough money to actually live on."

"You have some new clients for me?"

"I'm not talking about the tutoring. I'm talking about an actual job. If you were willing to use a temporary implant, they'd have no objection—"

"Not an option."

"Why not?" Anger sparked in Far's eyes; any attempt to hide it would have been alien to her. "I'm not going to argue with you about your aversion to implantation tech, I know that's no use." Knew that from long experience. "But a temporary one, Vaun? What's wrong with that? You wouldn't even have to tell anyone else—"

"And when I conveniently started making the kind of money that only comes from working at a caster place?" Most businesses these days would reject you out of hand as soon as they found out you didn't have an implant. A slurry of words: company culture, transparency, workflow. Who wouldn't want to hire an employee you never had to give a drug test, and whose productivity you could track just by sitting in the same room?

"Shit. This isn't how I wanted to tell you." She rolled over to the other side of the bed, waved the drawer of the nightstand open and dipped her hand into its darkness to withdraw a small glass vial with a dead worm inside. No, not dead; as she moved it towards me it gave a feeble twitch in its sterilizing liquid. Even from here I could see the way the mouth of the tube was shaped to fit perfectly against the socket of an eye, forming a perfect seal for the gel to settle against lid and lash before the digital tunneler did its work.

"It's a biodegradable model," Far said. In her voice, she had already won. "About a three-month half-life. They're actually *more* expensive than the permanent ones, you know. And if you'd just apply for a job that would cover—look. That doesn't matter. With this, I could have something lined up for you in a matter of days. Something that would actually pay. And I could help you. Tell you what to expect, coach you through the effects." She shifted closer. It struck me in a distant way that this little scene was exactly what Nan had probably envisioned when I told her I got a job in the city. She'd always said that corruption would be seductive.

I pulled away.

Before Far could reach for me, I was out of the bed, shoving various limbs into various articles of clothing, hoping I matched up the right holes.

"Vaun. Wait. *Wait.*" Far stumbled out of bed after me, flailing for a robe at its foot that she only managed to get half on. I couldn't tug my boots on before her hand settled on my shoulder. "Listen. I wasn't trying to offend you—"

"You have no idea what you're asking me to risk."

"God damnit, Vaun, that's because you never tell me!"

"There are plenty of things about me that you wouldn't understand."

"If you had the implant, I wouldn't have to—" She cut herself off before I could do it for her. Far's face was flushed. She didn't fight the tide of her anger. There was something comforting in knowing that for all the teeming life that existed beneath the surface of her, at least that surface couldn't lie.

"Alright," she said, and just like that the anger began to fade. "Alright. Just—this is an option, alright? I got it for *you*. And it'll be waiting, whether you change your mind or not."

I watched her cross the room and put the thing back into the drawer. When she turned to me, she didn't bother to pull her robe shut, and I didn't bother not to look.

"Stay a little longer?" she said. There were times when she really could speak like a natural. But even as she stepped forward and leaned in, my eyes stayed open, on that bedside drawer. Visions of her holding it over my eye socket as I slept played with the gruesome relish of a slasher film. When she pulled back, I couldn't shift my eyes back fast enough.

"Gotta get back," I said, and her mouth did that thing that was almost a smile. Casters never were good at faking expressions.

"I just want to help," she said, and that was the worst part.

I leaned in to kiss her again, closed-lipped right up until the end, because I knew I'd want to be back here and wouldn't want to spend the next time putting out the fires I left burning today. Her fingers curled in the fleece-lined collar of my jacket, the grip light and brittle as the dry curl of the thing in the vial. I let it linger before pulling away. I was pretty good at tolerating things by now.

I scrolled through Tocsin's messages as the train slid free of the glass sheath at the edge of the city and began to pick up speed. *On my way back. You good?* I waited five minutes, refreshing my handheld, before slipping its cool weight back into my pocket. I almost pinged

Tocsin's sister Coxcomb, but I knew better than to start asking around before I knew what Tocsin had gotten himself into.

The compound was only the last stop on the rail line in the loosest sense of the term. In reality you had to get off at the industrial district and walk another two miles down a road that was more weed than asphalt, cross-hatched with tar that could never hold the bursting cracks closed for long. Eventually you got to a chain link gate with a keypad—not exactly friendly, but we'd had our share of teenage casters prowling the perimeter, always in packs, silent, sometimes lobbing a rock or can of beer over the fence. No one else came out here, no one kept track of us, no one cared what was done to us or what we did to each other. I punched buttons so worn any idiot could probably guess the code, and stepped inside.

I could hear it before I saw it, the threads of noise breaking through the quiet like lightning in a summer storm. High raucous laughter, shouts of greeting or admonition, the clatter of doors and feet and conversations. I made my way down the central road through town, raising my hand to a few passing groundcars which honked at me as they crunched over the gravel. This time of day, most people were sitting out on their porches to watch the street, tinny songs blaring on their radios, the ice in their glasses clinking. More than a few had patches over their eyes.

The commotion on the Lin family's porch stopped me short before I reached my place. The usual crowd was gathered there, but today it didn't seem friendly. People lingered on the lawn to watch and listen and comment to their friends—arguments were a spectator sport. I couldn't make out the words, but I didn't really have to. I just had a hard time believing anyone in that household would have gone and put that thing in their head, knowing the consequences. I kept walking, grateful no one saw me and called me over to join them.

I had to be careful about sharing my opinion on this kind of thing. People tended to assume I was biased, seeing as I worked in the city and was probably halfway to contaminated as a result. Nan certainly seemed to think so.

The lights were on in my house as I made my way up the path, and I could hear the sound of clanging pots and voices inside, the familiar hiss of the old oven. Grandpa Heimal was in his chair on the porch, as he always was unless someone forgot to wheel him out. The socket of his left eye clung to the shadows like a cave. He'd been one of the early-adopters, and he'd paid for it. By the time talk of malfunctions started slipping past the NDAs and corporate cover-ups, the implant had scrambled Heimal's brain from the inside out.

Nan did what she could for him, and for the others she found who'd been through the same. I sometimes wondered whether she left his hollowed-out eye socket uncovered as a reminder to all the rest of us. That was certainly Nan's style. I squeezed his shoulder as I walked to the door, and murmured a quick *hullo, Grandpa* the way a Buddhist might turn the prayer wheels in passing.

From the moment I stepped inside, I was surrounded by warmth and light and familiar voices, so loud I could scarcely hear myself think as I took off my coat and my hat.

"Vauneant's back!" someone in the kitchen cried, and seconds later I was pelted at knee-height by a bundle of niece, grinning up at me from her grip around my knees.

"We're making lasagana!" Cispontine squealed.

I bent down to scoop her up, forcing an easy smile. "That's my favorite!"

"Vaun," my sister's voice called from the kitchen, "Get in here and make sure the vegetables don't burn."

Dutifully I trooped toward her voice, Cispontine on my hip. I could only glance at the stairs that led to the bedrooms before stepping into the kitchen. It was already packed in there, my cousin Snowbrowth fanning the smoke away from the detector, Cispontine's older sister sitting on the counter picking at the chips and dip, while uncle Groak tried to harangue her into helping peel vegetables.

"Did you hear about the Lins?" someone said in my ear, but no, I hadn't heard, and it was too loud to have it explained to me. Everyone was talking at once and I could hardly make out a word of it, and didn't need to try.

A couple times I checked my handheld. Still no response. I couldn't help but glance at the ceiling, the only thing which separated me from Tocsin's room. It seemed to sag toward me with the weight of whatever had happened. But I couldn't get away now without questions, and those could be dangerous around here.

At last, lasagna came out of the oven and the vegetables were oversalted, and Coxcomb finished doling out a healthy portion onto a plate and arranged it neatly on a tray.

"Take this up?" she said, as she always did, and for once I was glad to do it.

The stairs sighed under my boots as I made my way up. Nan's room made up the entire third floor, perched up top of the rest of the house like a watchtower. From up here you could see the entire compound, the endless green sprawl of forest and the glitter of the city on the horizon. Nan looked up from her work as I came in, her cane hooked on the edge of her workbench and small wire-frame glasses perched on her nose like something from an old digital film. She was the only person I knew alive who still used glasses; surgical eye correction was one modern amenity that the rest of us had all conceded to, but Nan said it was a manipulation of natural flesh, too close to changing who she was. Her glasses should have made her look sweet, old-fashioned; instead they focused her hard gaze into something that could have set the dried pages of Far's book alight.

I didn't look at the curtain in the back of the room, pulled closed against the makeshift surgery, and I didn't breathe through my nose. Still, the hint of chemicals prickled at my nose, imagined or not. This was the room where they did it—behind the curtain, the cot with disposable sheets and the blinking medical equipment, scrounged from outdated tech. Everything Nan might need to pull a long, biotech strand from a wayward eye socket. There was always a choice, of course, for anyone caught with an implant: take the operation or never come back.

"Nan," I said.

"Vauneant." She straightened, laying her soldering iron back in its cradle. I couldn't make sense of the wires and old-fashioned circuit boards in front of her. A piece of the temperature regulator, maybe. Nan was good at taking things apart and putting them back together to her own specifications. She'd been a doctor, before the compound; that fact had been one of the first to impress itself on my young mind. The use of old-fashioned computers, she'd taught herself out of necessity.

"Back from the city?" she said, with polite disapproval.

I stepped forward to put the tray on the table beside her. Her hair was the color of surgical steel where it caught the white light of her desk lamp. "Someone has to make sure those layabouts don't starve you."

Nan smiled, but her eyes still studied me the way they studied everyone. No one discussed the idea of moving her to a room downstairs. This had been her throne room as long as anyone could remember, and nothing short of death would unseat her from it.

Nan picked up the soldering iron again, and leaned over the pine-green circuit board. "Hear about the Lin boy?"

"Heard something happened. Not what."

A little line of smoke appeared from beneath the thin metal tool, curling up towards the hard shine of her glasses. She didn't specify, and I knew what that meant. What else of importance could happen to us here?

"It was just one of the temporaries, thank God," Nan said after a moment. "Just a matter of waiting for it to drain out of him. Still, the weakness revealed itself. His family will need to be diligent."

From what people told me of the time four decades ago, Nan had always been hard even when her face was soft. Maybe that was how she'd pulled this community around her like meat wrapped around bone, after she lost Heimal in all the ways that counted; and why our family out of all the rest was one of the few in the compound that hadn't turned up some wayward son or daughter who decided to put a biocomputer in their head. Ever since I'd gotten the job with Far, Nan had started looking at me like a sheep dog might look at a ewe with a limp.

"I'm sure they'll set him straight," I said, and Nan nodded, satisfied; she bent back over her workbench, and I knew I was dismissed.

Down the stairs once more, the air seemed easier to breathe. Tocsin's door was at the end of the hall, shut. I went to my room, loudly kicked off my boots, and made the rest of the way barefoot down the beaten-up runner. I knocked twice with one knuckle, soft as a branch tapping a window. There was no reply. I entered silently.

Tocsin lay in bed looking like he should be in the middle of an impact crater. He blinked up at me, barely able to raise his head as I closed the door softly behind me. He looked as young as he'd been when we rode down the stairs on our pillows, and as shell-shocked as when his head met the bottom bannister.

One of his eyes was bruised, the white of it gone painfully red.

"Hey, Vaun," he croaked.

I let out a slow breath as I settled next to him on the bed. For a minute we just sat there, turning over the silence between us like it was a puzzle that together we could somehow pick apart.

"Sure hope you didn't let anyone see you looking like that," I said after a while.

"I'm not an idiot, thanks."

"Would a smart person go and do what you just did?"

"I needed the work. *We* needed it," Tocsin said. Though we kept our voices low, I could hear the bitterness creeping in at the edges.

"At least tell me it's temporary."

"How the hell was I supposed to afford one of those?"

I put my head in my hands. "God damnit, Tocsin."

"What else could I do, huh? How long am I supposed to sit around all day watching Mom and Coxcomb live off canned protein and nutrient pills because none of us can get a job?"

"You think they'd be happier to know you went and did the one thing Nan would run you out of here for? You know the rules, Tocsin—"

"Yes, I know, *Jesus*, I know." Tocsin put a hand over his eyes, hiding the inflamed one from view. "I just need to make enough money to get by on for a while. Then I'll turn it off, and no one will ever need to know." He lowered his hands to look at me with an expression of wheedling accusation. "You know I would have found your kind of work if I could."

I turned away, hating to hear him say that. I was the example every parent in our compound told their kids about—Vaun who had found work in the city and still managed to stay unpolluted. My life was better in theory than in practice. Without the welfare checks and the fact that I wasn't paying rent, I'd never be able to keep my head above water.

"Listen," Tocsin said. He picked at the stray thread of his cuff instead of looking at me. "Nan is going to start to ask questions about the money this job is going to bring in. I was hoping you could—you know. Spread it around that I got work with your people. To help explain it."

I nodded, but because he wasn't looking, I had to force my dead tongue to move. "Of course. Don't even ask me that."

"Thanks." His voice was flat. Not ungrateful; just tired.

I cleared my throat. "You going to go to the support group?"

"It's called intunement, but yeah."

Indoctrination, as Nan would put it. Still, I was glad. We were in a distinct position out here to know how bad a mind could go once the implant cracked it open.

I made a vague gesture at his face. "How long will all that last?"

"Should fade by morning."

"Better hope it does," I said, knowing he knew I would cover for him if it hadn't. I thought of Nan's hard eyes drilling into my head, the curtain and the smell of disinfectant; and also of the warm currents of talk and food and companionship that made this place a home. I'd seen what had happened to other kids when their families found out they strayed; either an empty eye socket or an empty place at the table. In a way our world was defined by absence as much as Far's was by the lack thereof. Was it better to be mutilated in body, or soul?

For a while longer I sat there. Then I rose, unable to stay another minute in that close room with its prickling silence, wondering what Tocsin was hearing and feeling that I just couldn't reach. The truth was, I was scared for him. But I had no idea how to tell him that, and in the end it was easier to say nothing at all.

"It's not a cult."

Sitting at our customary bench, Far turned to me with a wry smile. "You're good with words, Vaun. But I'm not confident in your ability to reason that one out."

"I don't have to convince you that I'm *not* in a cult. The burden of proof is on you."

"Fine." Far passed me her cig, which glowed brown this time. I eyed it nervously, but inhaled all the same. The cinnamon tasted like vague relief. Kite's lessons had been going well for the past couple weeks, and the latest tutoring lesson had ended early. Far had yet to ask me back to hers today. I think maybe part of her enjoyed the illicit thrill of sitting in public and *talking*. That irritated me a bit, but the fact was I liked talking to her.

She hadn't brought up the vial waiting in her bedside drawer again, either. I'd checked, once, while she was in the bathroom—it was still there. It could afford to wait.

Far held up a finger. "You live on a compound. You distrust outsiders. You reject modern technology for religious reasons—"

"It's not religion," I said, a little too sharply. I didn't like the way she was ticking my life off on her fingers like plot points in a hack novel.

Far looked at me, calculating. "You can believe in something religiously without any sort of God coming into it."

I looked away, biting the inside of my cheek. "You forgot to mention the human sacrifice," I said, and Far laughed that ugly sawing laugh of hers that I'd reluctantly come to enjoy.

It wasn't as if I hadn't thought about it, I almost wanted to say. The doors that would open for me as soon as I let the world into my thoughts would change my life forever. But it would mean shutting another door behind me, the one which led to the only family and home I'd ever known. Birthed into the amniotic ocean of thought as she'd been, I didn't think Far could understand that.

"Come on," she said, slipping the cig back into her breast pocket. "It's a beautiful day. Let's walk to my place for once."

"You're assuming I want to come home with you."

"Yes, I am."

I rolled my eyes, a gesture that Far had never succeeded in duplicating. I ought to have told her I had somewhere to be, just to prove that I could still say no, but in the end the flesh was weak.

As we left the park, I was immediately glad to have Far at my side. Hanging trolleys whispered over our heads as they passed, sweeping over the shuffle of hundreds of feet and the soft hush of cars sliding past. The faces which passed were alight with a wash of silent emotion. The buildings were paneled with blank screens, grim and grey—only a caster could perceive what they were trying to sell.

There were others here, I knew, who had once been like me. Expats from the compound who'd kept their eyes and implants, and lost everything else. None had ever approached me. They'd been subsumed, just a few more silent ghosts wandering the city streets.

"Doesn't it bother you?" I asked. My words smeared that silence like an obscene stain. "The quiet."

Far snorted, tossing her long braid over her shoulder. She made more seemingly unconscious sound than any other caster I had met. I wonder if the people around her thought her strange, or whether she could turn it on and off as easily as a switch in her head. "I could ask you the same question."

"And I'd tell you that it does. It bothers me a lot."

She shrugged. "It isn't quiet for me. I can cast into the thoughts of people around me, if I want to. Except yours."

"That sounds awful."

"Oh, I'm sure I'm not missing out on much." She sobered a little, turning to face me with her full interest. "The idea of walking around with cotton stuffed in my brain, numb and dumb to everyone—*that* sounds awful to me."

"Maybe I like keeping some things to myself."

"Interesting use of conditional, considering you're the most covert person I know. You'd tell me if you were some kind of murderer, right?"

"Depends. Can you keep a secret?"

Far laughed again, and then covered her mouth when a person passing us looked at her sharply. It was rude to break the quiet, and I felt a little good about that; like I'd managed to show her something about me, without even really trying. I supposed that to venture out of the city and into that vast silence where there was nothing to cast to or to cast back at you would be a kind of death to Far. A terrible thing, to be cut off from all you'd ever known.

Then she leaned over to peck my cheek, and I stopped thinking about unreachable worlds for a while.

"I really do want to know."

Far said this before I'd started getting dressed again, which was how I knew she might be serious. "Why is rejecting the implant so important to you and yours?" she continued, on seeing I was listening.

I propped myself up on a hand, thinking. She'd never asked before, not really, so I'd never had to explain it before. I thought about what Nan would say: that language made us human, and the implants made us something else. Having seen the city, it was hard to argue with that. But there was something more to it; something even Far might understand.

"Have you ever asked someone where they wanted to eat dinner, listened to them think aloud about what they're in the mood for, until you can both agree on something? Or do you just think *food* and pick up the general sensations and cravings of the person you're with?"

"I don't see the difference. We end up at the restaurant either way."

"There's no room for mistakes. For all the little things you lose and gain between thought to word to thought again."

Far raised her eyebrows. "Translations are imperfect by nature."

"Art is an imperfect translation."

"Now you're just being pretentious."

"Now I'm trying to make a *point*."

That familiar smile touched half her lips. "If only you had an implant. Imagine how easily you could convey your ideas."

It was a joke. It should have been easy to laugh it off. But I couldn't just then; I was thinking about Tocsin, and my grandfather's eye drifting like a dead log on a placid sea. When my gaze slid to Far again, her own face had gotten quiet.

"Vaun," she said. "If there were something bad happening out there, would you tell me?"

I pressed a kiss to the back of her hand in lieu of an answer, but in the end she took it as answer enough.

When I reached the final train stop within the city limits, the car emptied as if disemboweled. It was only me and an older woman who sat at the end, veined hands trembling over her handscreen. As soon as we passed a certain stop, a switch was triggered—now the spilling color over the walls had sound attached, music that poured out of the train's tinny speakers and startled me into alertness.

"With new implant technology, it's never been easier to upgrade," a cheerful baritone said as images flashed across the screen—people effortlessly finding each other across a crowded train station, a team of dancers coordinating in a complex routine, a mother casting at her baby for the first time. *"The world is waiting. Cast out for it."*

The ads were clearly targeted. In the end, no one would even have to force us—it would just happen slowly, as people gave in, realized it was easier to assimilate, told themselves they'd stay vocal with their families, their kids; but how many generations would it take for even that faint conviction to flicker out?

Glancing at the old woman at the other end of the train, I realized she was staring at me hard—and that she was probably trying to cast at me. When the train reached its final stop I got off quickly, leaving her behind.

The walk back to the compound went quickly, lost in my thoughts as I was. The sound of raised voices from beyond the chain link fence didn't strike me as particularly alarming until the gate rolled back on its aging motor and I saw the crowd.

They were gathered outside of my house.

I didn't realize I was running until the scene wavered and dragged me closer like something from a bad dream. No elbowing through the crowd tonight; people saw me and they split apart. Even from the outskirts I could see Nan on the porch, leaning on her walking stick. She only ever came down the stairs in a crisis. Now that crisis was seething around my home like antibodies around a virus.

And then Nan's eyes shifted to me, and nothing in her expression or posture changed; it was just that I bore the full weight of her attention like the muzzle of a gun held inches from my forehead. People were asking her questions, asking *me* questions, but all I could do was stand there skewered by her gaze. I knew she knew I'd kept Tocsin's secrets, and that made me hardly any better than him.

I cleared the porch steps in two strides, my eyes shifting from Nan to the door. I just had to get to Tocsin. But before I could step forward, a hand shot out to catch my arm in a grip you'd only use on an animal, something whose pain didn't need respecting. Behind her glasses, Nan's eyes bored into mine.

"It's done," she said. I tried to tear away, but she held me fast. "We gave him the choice," Nan said, each word another chunk bitten out of me. "He chose *us.*"

I was not deaf to the inference, the silent second half of her sentence: the choice that I had made, without ever knowing I had made it. I stared into Nan's eyes, but they were flat behind the glass. I thought of Coxcomb and Cispontine and Groak, the noise and love and connection. No one stepped forward to speak for me now. The silence around me bled like a wound.

Nan let me go. I stumbled, nearly fell into someone; I didn't see or care who. The door, the house—someone tried to stop me, but I heard Nan's voice. "Let her say her goodbyes. She'll be gone within the hour."

I turned on her. Numbness spread through my chest like a branching tree of dead nerves. "I should get a choice," I said, my voice hollow. "You give everyone a choice."

Nan shook her head. "You already made it."

I turned around. The house was empty as a tomb. Up the stairs. My eyes stung and swam, but I kept moving. Tocsin's door was open, vacant. It was Nan's room I went to; the door was unlocked, the computer parts on the workbench all filed into the separate compartments of her plastic storage container. The curtain on the other side of the room had been drawn back. I saw the bright red biohazard bin first, the color snagging my eye. The blink of the machines: pulse, breath, things that made no sense to me. Half of Tocsin's face had a piece of medical gauze taped over it, and where once the eye had lain beneath it there was a rose of blood budding in the cotton, unfurling with each beep of the machines. Still sedated. We weren't barbarians, tearing out the eyes of our unwilling victims without proper medical procedure. That was the worst of it, of course—that in the end, Tocsin had chosen this. As much as you could choose anything, when the alternative was to be stripped of everything you'd ever known and loved.

I sat by his bedside a long time, knowing he wouldn't wake for hours. Even if he had, I knew what he'd probably say.

No one tried to stop me as I left. They went silent as I passed. I spread it around me like a stench. The sun was going down, and there were no lights on the long cracked road back to the train station. In the dark, all I could see was the spot of blood. I knew I'd never walk this road again. What was wrong with me wasn't something they could pluck out.

I sat on the steps to Far's building for a long time, waiting for her to see my message. I'd only sent the one; I couldn't dig up the words, the urgency, the hour, the year. I didn't know how I'd found my way here, other than following something I hadn't known was inside of me. The city was utterly silent but for the occasional sound of footsteps. It didn't bother me now. I never wanted to hear a spoken word again.

When the door behind me opened I jerked like someone caught nodding off. And then Far was in front of me, her arms gripping her elbows. Her eyes were confused, and a little scared, and darted between me and the heavy backpack leaning against my leg.

"Um." I followed her gaze to my pack. For a moment I lost myself in its shape and contours, which seemed more real to me than anything else had ever been in my life. It occurred to me in a distant way that this might be asking too much; that Far might actually turn me away. "I know you don't have any reason to—"

"Get in here," she said with hoarse exasperation, as if there had never been any other answer at all. She led me to her door, or she must have—I didn't feel awake or alive in the strictest sense of the word. Eventually I was naked, in her bed, and she was molded to me, chaste and still clothed. For once, I wanted to tell her everything. I wanted to open my mouth and let it pour out of me like bile dredged up from deeper than retching should go. My tongue was stone. I smelled disinfectant on every breath.

I reached for the gleam before my eyes, the single point of light: the metal knob of the bedside table that I had opened a hundred times in my mind. Far's hand tangled with mine before I could fumble inside. She pulled my hand back and pressed it to my chest until I could feel every beat of my heart as clearly as if I held it in the palm of my hand.

"Shh," she said, and stroked my hair. "Shh."

And for a while there was silence deeper than I had ever known, and in Far's arms I drank from it until I was full.

"Lingua Franca" originally appeared in *Metaphorosis*
on 16 October 2020.

About the author

Amelia Fisher has more plants, postcards, and half-finished stories than are probably good for her. She writes queer speculative fiction from her home amidst the moss and gloom of the Pacific Northwest.

ameliafisher.com, @hubristicfool

Rekindled

Mikko Rauhala

Nera knew something was amiss as soon as she noticed the crow cooing on her porch a mere three weeks after the fall equinox. Mother's next letter, no doubt wishing Nera well in all her endeavors, wasn't due until the winter solstice.

The crow cawed and pushed a small container tied to his leg toward Nera.

"Just a moment, Wisp. I'll get you your treat," she said to the crow. Intelligent as the familiar was, he was still a crow. Headstrong, willful, proud—just as Mother liked it. He would run errands for her, to be sure, but he expected to be properly compensated for his time and effort.

Wisp bobbed his head up and down in acknowledgment. Nera entered her single-room hut, suitable for an independent medicine woman in her late twenties. A simple stone fireplace in the corner to keep her warm, a bed to let her rest her bones, and a stool and a table to write on. A shelf to the left of the fireplace held jars of herbs and tinctures of various kinds, and the shelf to the right was reserved for more mundane foodstuffs. She reached into a jar on the latter shelf, pulled out a handful of nuts, and returned outside.

She crouched next to Wisp, placed the nuts on the porch, and said: "Here you go. Could I have Mother's letter now, please?"

The crow tilted his head, a gesture that Nera had learned to take for a smile, and proceeded to tinker with the string on his leg. As soon as he'd gotten the container free, he picked it up and placed it on Nera's hand. Then he turned to regard the pile of nuts.

"Could you wait a while so I can see if an immediate reply is called for?"

Wisp picked up a nut in his beak, bobbed his head up and down, and proceeded to bite into the treat.

"Thanks," Nera said with a smile. "I'll try to make it quick." Then she went inside and opened the window next to the table. The sun was still high, and the southwestern view was good for evening reading.

Nera popped the container's cap, dug out a small scroll, and spread it onto the table. Despite her age, Mother's hand was as steady as ever. Nera had to squint to make out the tiny letters:

Dear Nera,

I hope this letter finds you well. It occurs to me that we've barely spoken anything of import for the better part of the decade. I'd like for us to get to know each other again, and give Wisp some proper exercise. What say you?

Regards,

Raziela

Nera chuckled. This was a change from the formal pleasantries they usually exchanged four times a year. Not an unwelcome one, though. They'd just sort of drifted apart since Mayview had lost its previous medicine woman and Nera had answered the call. But maybe it was time to reconnect.

Dipping her pen in the inkwell, Nera wrote her agreement on the blank side of the scroll, then rolled the message back into the cylinder. Wisp jumped up on the table, having eaten his fill, and Nera tied the message to his leg. "Thanks, Wisp. Give Mother my best," she said.

Wisp cawed and took off through the open window, disappearing into the sun.

Two days later the crow returned, and twice a week hence. The pace was such that it was all Nera could do to think of something to write back before Wisp would be knocking on her door again.

Mother shared her memories of the early years, how she'd juggled raising a baby and serving her community, not always to her own satisfaction. She wrote about how she'd kept Nera busy with learning about healing herbs and tinctures as soon as she was out of the crib. She recounted how distraught she'd been when the whooping cough had spread throughout the village, Nera falling ill among the rest, but how her medicinal arts had managed to triumph over it in the end.

And she wrote of the bittersweet sensation of Nera coming into her own and leaving for Mayview, of her regret over letting their contact largely lapse while busying herself in her own responsibilities. Nera sent a reply reminding her that they'd both had their hand in that.

As the year marched on and the winter solstice approached, Mother suggested that Nera join her for a quiet celebration. Nera happily agreed and prepared for the journey.

Nera's old home was as it had ever been. The stone house was twice the size of Nera's own, and had twice the rooms—gratitude of a village well served. A diverse herb garden dominated the front yard, its lushness only slightly reined in by the mild winter air. The rest of the surroundings were as nature wished.

A caw from above welcomed her as she approached the front door by way of the narrow garden path. Nera looked up and saw Wisp circling in the sky. She gave him a little wave, and the crow dove down and in through a cracked window at the front.

"Ah, she's here?" asked a familiar voice from her childhood. There was an affirmative caw. "Come on in!" Mother hollered. "It's not as if I've put a bolt on the door!"

Nera chuckled. "Didn't expect you had!" The hinges creaked with age as she opened the door to the main room. It hadn't changed a bit since Nera last laid eyes on it, except for the large piles of paper in every corner of the room. The walls were otherwise lined with shelves full of one odd thing or another. To the left of the door stood a table with some dishes and cutlery on it. A tattered couch lay near the fireplace.

The door to her mother's room was open, not that there was any chance of closing it without clearing some of the clutter first. Nera peeked in, barely catching sight of Wisp's tail at the window as he took off into the air again. Mother sat at her desk with a pile of empty papers on her left and full ones on her right, her quill furiously working on the half-filled sheet in front of her.

Mother raised her smiling face toward Nera, but her hand continued scribbling as she spoke: "Welcome, welcome, my child. It's good to see you after so long."

"Too long, Mother. It's good to see you, and that you're as vital as ever. It's not just my correspondence keeping your hand busy, then?" Nera asked, trying to insert some levity into the obvious question.

Mother's smile widened. "No, it's not. But it is one of my more pleasant pastimes."

"What're you working on now?" Nera asked.

"Come and have a look, why don't you?"

Nera came closer and tilted her head to get a better view of her mother's writing:

Nera came closer and tilted her head to get a better view of my writing, said the latest line of text as soon as her mother had finished with it. Nera raised her eyebrow. *Nera raised her eyebrow*, Mother added.

Nera sat on the spare stool next to the desk. "Well, at least from what I can tell, you're writing what I'm doing *after* the fact," she said matter-of-factly.

Her mother chuckled. "Right you are, my girl. You always were quick to notice such things." Her hand continued to write. A quick glance told Nera that yes, her mother was writing her own words down as well.

"For what purpose are you narrating everything we do, if you don't mind me asking?"

"Why, what does one usually make notes for? I want to be able to remember my dear daughter's visit. Ah. 'Nera pursed her lips, perhaps thinking my memory isn't what it used to be.' My recollection is fine, dear. It's just, you know, sometimes writing things down helps in forming memories. Ones that last."

"I see." What with the piles of text in the house, Nera wondered if her mother's scribal habits had gotten a bit out of control. Then again, Mother seemed very present even as her hand wrote down the minutiae of their encounter. Perhaps she should reserve judgment. "Well, if you think my visit is worth jotting down, who am I to argue?" She gave her mother a smile.

"Worth it indeed. Now, if you wouldn't mind lending a hand, we should probably be getting ready for supper, and I've had my hands full in writing my memoirs. I do have some sweets stashed for the solstice, so fear not, it'll be more than potatoes."

Nera laughed, and they proceeded to the main room to prepare supper, mother taking her quill and some sheets along.

As they dug into their vegetable casserole at the table, Mother noted that she'd want to know all about Nera's life in Mayview, everything Nera hadn't had time to go through yet in their correspondence.

Mother dipped her quill in ink and made notes as Nera recounted some of her older trials and triumphs from back when she'd just started out on her own. Easing births, setting bones, pulling teeth. More often than not, she'd managed to eke out a victory for life, and from the occasional defeat she'd made a point to learn what went wrong, to better be prepared for the next challenge.

Given a less-than-subtle prod from her mother, Nera mused that there was, indeed, a man in the village who'd been casting eyes at her. However, she was doing just fine on her own, and she'd kept away from such attentions thus far as she wasn't certain that was quite her thing. Mother laughed at that, telling the blushing Nera that she didn't have to have any one thing if she didn't so choose, or, indeed, any thing at all.

The two talked well into the night, taking a break only to go outside and see the midnight stars as they were on the darkest night of the year. Eventually the late hour got the better of them, and they fell asleep together in Mother's bed.

The next day it was time for Nera to leave, as it was not good for a medicine woman to stay away from her village for too long. The two exchanged hearty goodbyes, and promised to continue keeping Wisp busy.

Nera left for home, her step heavy only for the voluminous pages of medicinal lore her mother had bestowed on her, fresh out of the quill.

Three weeks after her visit, Nera woke up to a loud cawing from the door. Everything was dark, and Nera felt that she hadn't had a proper night's sleep. Wisp must've flown to her across the night. That was unusual, to say the least.

She rose to sit and fumbled for the lantern and tinderbox by her bedside. Getting a flame going was a moment's work. Then she dragged her feet to the door and opened it.

Wisp was standing on the porch, his head low, with a cylinder that must've been ten inches long beside him. There was no string, though the cylinder had a couple of clawholds.

"Oh, my. You've been brave," Nera said.

Wisp ruffled his feathers and stepped inside wearily, leaving the cylinder out on the porch.

"I'll take care of that for you," Nera said, picking up the package and closing the door. "You must be starving. Let me get you a little something before I open this."

Wisp cawed approvingly as Nera set some nuts and dried berries on a plate in front of him. Then she sat on her desk and opened the cylinder in the light of the lantern.

Out popped a single scroll along with a black quill pen, similar to what her mother had used when Nera was visiting. She examined the quill in her hand. The feather had perfect vanes with a smooth shine to them. The tip was sharp, suitable for precision work. Such quills were often from crows.

"This yours?" Nera asked Wisp.

The familiar cawed and bobbed his head up and down.

"From a molting, I trust?" she continued. That was, after all, the usual way.

Wisp nodded again, then turned back to his nuts.

Nera flashed a brief smile. "A considerate gift, to be sure, but you wouldn't have had to fly all night to bring it," she said as she laid the pen down on the table and spread out the scroll.

Dear Nera,

I thank you for a truly blessed time these past few months. Our correspondence has been a wonderful way for me to reminisce, to take stock of my life through writing. I must confess I had an ulterior motive for this, but do not doubt my sincerity in everything I've written, for it was a necessity in fulfilling my other purpose as well. I'm proud of you, and though I taught you to be a medicine woman, I fear I may have concentrated on that overmuch, leaving you to teach yourself to be a proper human being. It is of some consolation that you've done a good job of it.

I have lived a good, long life, and I could feel it in my bones that this would be my last winter. So I poured out my soul through this here quill, to keep it when my body was done.

That time has come. Please take care of Wisp for me, and arrange a proper burial for my earthly remains. All of my wisdom, such as it is, is yours to find in my writings at home.

Or you may find it in your hand, as I am here for you, if you'll have me.

Love,

The letter ended without a signature.

After staring at the scroll for a few moments, Nera became aware of movement in her peripheral vision and turned to look. The quill was hovering over the inkwell in a quiet gesture of request, rotating as if suspended from above by a thread. Nera's mouth fell open.

Moving as if in a dream, she opened the inkwell. The pen carefully dipped in, swooped up to the letter and signed it: *Raziela.* Mother's handwriting, no doubt about it.

Wisp hopped onto the table and nuzzled Nera. She pushed back softly, her eyes still on the hovering quill. Wisp hopped over her arm and nuzzled the quill, which caressed his feathers gently. Wisp tilted his head contentedly.

A single tear rolled down Nera's cheek.

"Welcome home, Mom."

"Rekindled" originally appeared in *Community of Magic Pens*
on 4 May 2020.

About the author

Mikko Rauhala is a bilingual Finnish SF author, and a vegan since the turn of the millennium. In "Rekindled", their Best Vegan SFF story, they endeavoured to include a sympathetic animal character with agency of his own. Rauhala's debut collection *Infinite Metropolis* (Aurelia Leo, 2020), co-authored with Edmund Schluessel, represents their more science fictional work. They can be reached at rauhala.org, and they tweet at @AuthorRauhala

Seven Scraps Unwritten

L. Chan

Scrap 1: Monograph on the four catechisms

The first catechism of Eulalia is DIVERSITY LEADS TO STRENGTH. Its sigil is a square made of four interlocked components, reminiscent of hands each grasping the wrist of the next, forming a box.

Scrap 1 has an annotation, handwritten: This logos is one of the most complex in the Logocracy of Eulalia. This and the other three logos are said to be without beginning, just as the Logocracy is without beginning. The scholarship of history needs to cut through this jingoism – even mountains have beginnings; so too our Logocracy. Any logos starts by erasing the parchment or substrate beneath it. What was erased to create Eulalia? To give way to the Logocracy?

Scrap 2: Transcript of the thesis defence of Thera

Thera: The Conceit in the Republic of Eulalia is not illusion, although most people think it is. The magic of Eulalia is delusion; instead of seeing things that aren't there, people believe things are there that are not. Consider the walls of the University. We do not need to paint them as other nations do; a trained logomancer needs only to scribe the logos for red upon them, and if enough people believe that the walls are red, everyone will.

Third chair: Apprentice Thera, you seek to ascend to Journeyer and you present the pap that we feed to children in school.

Thera: I present the converse, that the principle can be reversed. There is an antithesis to logomancy, and its roots are within what I just explained. What if the opposite could be achieved: that things could be uncreated, not by the delusion of the many but by the will of the few?

Seventh chair: A decade's worth of study, and you bring to us debunked theses, Journeyer. Your thesis defence need not proceed.

Thera: I am due my hour, honoured chair. The charter guarantees it, and I claim this right. We are unique amongst the kingdoms, alone in our system of rule, lasting as long as the other kingdoms but without strife and struggle. The same charter that keeps the peace and establishes the ten Chairs gives me an hour.

Seventh chair: Look how she demands. We should never have taken a mongrel 'mancer like you into the University. The Book of Lies is a myth;

something for separatists and agitators and ingrates who do not value the gifts of Eulalia.

Thera: I did not mention the Book of Lies, honoured seventh.

Seventh chair: I'll not have you being smart-mouthed with a Chair, you backwoods child.

Tenth chair: Thera is my student, seventh. We are here to question her theories, not her lineage.

Seventh chair: No need to remind, Tenth; we would have known her as yours from her debasement of orthodoxy. Always abusing your discretion to bring us those furthest from the ways of the Logomancy. And encouraging them towards spurious inquiry.

Scrap 2 ends here. The full transcript has been forcefully torn out of University thesis records. Only this page survives. The scribe has no recollection of the exchange.

Scrap 3: 4th year Academic Report of Journeyer Thera

Journeyer Thera is but a middling student – a level belying her intellect. Her work, when she does apply herself, is brilliant. In her third year, she rather elegantly conjoined two obscure logos to solve a term problem at least a fifth more efficiently than the model answer. Had she handed in her solution on time, she would be in line for an academic prize and her choice of supervisors at the Academy.

In outlook, she is prone to distraction. She uses twice as much paper and ink as the next student, and most of it wasted on half scribbled proofs. Thera imbibes far too freely of the student presses, addled by dangerous thought when she isn't dashing her head out against ancient unsolved logos. A dreamer and not a completionist, and unlikely to go far in Logomancy.

I beseech you, honoured Proctor, not to accede to the Academy's assigned supervisor. She has done nothing to warrant being assigned a master of any note, let alone the Tenth Chair. Tell them that she is ill, that a tragedy has befallen her family. Were she to demonstrate her incompetence to the Tenth Chair, our department would be a laughing stock for years.

Scrap 4: Banned playbill circulated across the Academy campus

LIES LIES LIES LIES

THE LOGOCRACY IS NOT BUILT ON THE CATECHISMS. IT IS BUILT ON LIES. WHAT OF THE SHORTAGE, WHAT OF THE RIOTS, WHAT OF THE MASSACRES?

WHAT OF THE MISSING?

THE BOOK OF LIES IS REAL. THE BOOK OF LIES TAKES AWAY OUR HISTORY, OUR FRIENDS. THE FOUNDATIONS ARE FALSE. THE CHAIRS ARE COMPLICIT. EVEN THE TENTH.

LIES LIES LIES

A scrawled message on the reverse:

"Esteemed Tenth, the penmanship on the playbill is rather brutish; mayhap it has roots far from our fair capital? You grow nostalgic as your time wanes, sweet Tenth. Your protégé reminds me much of you in your youth. We value original thought, but within reasonable bounds: a lesson you have yet to teach young Thera. A warning from one chair to another, school young Thera quickly, lest the First chair withdraw your prerogative to choose your successor."

Scrap 5: The Rules of Succession of Eulalia, An Intercepted Dispatch from the H.E. Elevier, Emissary of the Empire Sound

The High Chair is rotated amongst the ten Chairs of the Logocracy, in the order of their numbers, each ruling a year in turn. Nine of the ten chairs have not changed since we started keeping records in Sound. They are immortal, but not like the Undying Queen of Dark Under The Mountain, who rules from her crystal sarcophagus. Some craft protects nine chairs, the easiest guess being logomancy, although the logos for immortality must then be a closely guarded secret. It would be of great import to the Emperor were we able to procure it.

Only the tenth chair changes. The means of succession are opaque. Once, at a formal dinner a month ago I asked the Fourth chair, a woman of startling plainness and skinnier than a broom handle, what purpose this served. She replied that hubris accretes to immortality like rust to old iron, and only the Tenth chair keeps them all honest. Influence could be brought to bear, if only we knew how they chose the Tenth. I sought the Tenth at the dinner, but could not procure an opportunity to speak with him; his evening was taken up by a young lady, broad shouldered and dark, from warmer climes. If there were reason for a simple student to be at a dinner thrown by the Logocracy, it is lost on me.

Nevertheless, elements of unrest also exist in Eulalia, albeit under control. Insurgency could weaken Eulalia and be to our benefit, but Eulalia is frustratingly stable. More so than her neighbours with the same constraints of rain and crop, but absent the force of arms that would quell protest. Dissidents whisper of some branch of logomancy that we've not yet seen, something that erases instead of creates. Perhaps this is even more valuable than the secret of the nine chairs.

I have another minor complaint against our historians – the schooling provided to me about Eulilian history was far from accurate. For example, the reported riots amidst the famine two score years ago don't seem to have happened at all. The same with the attempted annexure of West Eulalia by our Empire seventy-six years ago. Nobody in the country remembers these, even amongst those with no love for the Logocracy. The further from home I get, the more ridiculous these histories sound. I tried to find them in the précis given to all Empire diplomats, but they seem to have gone. It appears the air itself in Eulalia cannot stomach lies like this.

Scrap 5 ends here. Elevier was known to have subsequently divorced his Empire wife, and settled down in the Eulalian capital for the rest of his life. He never left the city and continued to draw a modest but adequate pension from the Empire. He never communicated with his embassy again.

Scrap 6: Requisition chit for additional workmen for renovation works on the Academy Library

Name: Eksbrys, Sub-Chair of Library
          Management

To: Department of Works, Fourth Chair

Date: 21st Day of Winterterm

Order: 4 workmen from the Department of
          Conservation, to restore a partially
          collapsed wall in the library.

Scrap 6: Written on the overleaf of the chit, in the different writing. "As a sub-chair, you should have known to pay attention to works around the Folded Library. You know that the Book is inscribed on the walls within. Were it not for the quick actions of the Journeyer studying in the Folded Library, the men would have left with their memories intact, to great mischief. Still, a more permanent solution is needed. The Book must take care of them. You will see to pensions and compensation to their families – Second Chair."

Scrap 7: Excerpt from a graded assignment, submitted by Journeyer Athyl

Eulalian society is based on four simple rules; four catechisms each represented by a logos. The catechisms themselves are of breath-taking complexity; none but the most talented logomancers can even dream of scribing one, and their services are always in demand.

The craft of Logomancy turns towards the continued evolution of all our logos, the paring of superfluous lines, collapsing form until purer intent remains. Yet research on the four base logos of our society is forbidden by the ten chairs. Their forms remain archaic, with nested logos adding to needless intricacy.

That the ten chairs take such pains to develop the craft of Logomancy elsewhere, but forbid it on the catechisms is telling. That the law has been in place since the establishment of the positions of chairs suggests that the longevity of our means of government is linked to our catechisms. After all, our magic is based on delusion and what more powerful delusion is there than our belief in the catechisms?

So armed, I sought to dissect one of the logos representing the first catechism, and there it was – a subtle work, echoed in the other three catechisms: ancient sublogos speaking to life and regrowth, turned towards the continued rule of the chairs. In seeing the way out of one problem, I have found another. There is no reason why the magic could not go ten ways instead of nine.

While we remember the names of the tenth chairs through to the current, there has never been a death celebration for a single one. While not prone to the wilder theories circulating about the Academy campus, I cannot help but wonder at the potential for a double tragedy, that the tenth chair, with the opportunity to learn the secrets I've found here, has the opportunity to change the system and never does. Has the opportunity to grasp immortality but never does. Has the opportunity to die as the rest of us do, but is just another victim of the Book of Lies.

Scrap 7, Handwritten comments:

Dear Athyl, this is a promising start to your final year at the academy, but this paper should be rewritten in a less controversial manner, and perhaps one which less excoriates your thesis supervisor. You are right about more things than you know now, and headstrong, and hopeful. All the reasons why I chose you, all the reasons I was chosen.

The nine have hidden their power in the basic foundations of our country, but more terrifying is their power to erase, to make us forget. Even ascension is paid for by a tithe of memory, but we never forget hope. Even after they have unwritten what I was, I see in you what I hoped to be.

I invite you to join me in the library after hours. My name to the guards will see you in. Your craft has a ways to go before you can call yourself logomancer, but your mind can no longer be sharpened by the classroom. Your instruction will continue in the Folded Library, as mine once did.

Your Supervisor, Tenth Chair Thera.

"Seven Scraps Unwritten" originally appeared in Metaphorosis
on 17 April 2020.

About the author

L. Chan hails from Singapore. He spends most of his time wrangling two dogs. His work has appeared in places like *Translunar Travellers Lounge, Podcastle,* and *the Dark,* and he was a finalist for the 2020 Eugie Foster Memorial Award. He tweets occasionally @lchanwrites.

lchanwrites.wordpress.com

The First Step in Our Evolution

Marisca Pichette

Jenji held her fan delicately, her nails reflecting the sun. With short, stiff motions she directed the feather forward. It levitated once, twice, jumping the sticks I'd laid out as obstacles. My fan was folded, pinched tight in my sweating hands as I watched her feather pull ahead of mine.

The dry breeze blew her feather out of bounds. "Crap," Jenji said. I couldn't help myself as I grinned, unfolding my fan.

"My turn."

I inched forward on my stomach, dust grinding between my knees and the ground. The sun burned my scalp. Unlike Jenji, I'd forgotten my hat. Now the summer sun baked the back of my neck, my nose, and my arm as I reached out, my fan nudging the air.

It wobbled up, floating over the second stick. I flicked my wrist to keep it airborne; if it touched the ground, my turn was forfeited back to Jenji, and I had a feeling she would win on her next go.

Flick. Flick. My feather passed the third stick. Only one more separated mine from Jenji's.

I dragged myself forward, uselessly wetting my chapped lips. Faha told me it only made them drier, and took away some of my own regulated hydration. I knew she was right; my mother's courtesans were always right. That didn't keep me from doing it, though.

Sweat crept down my back. I looked at Jenji. She was a few years older than me, my only friend in the villa. Her face was free from moisture, a new normal that I was still getting used to.

I looked back at my progress too late. My feather touched the ground.

Jenji threw her fan open with a snap. She tipped her hat back on her head and started waving. In a matter of seconds, the game was over. She'd won, as usual.

We walked back to the villa side by side, looking forward to cups of jade green cactus juice and sliced pineapple. Sure enough, Faha and some of the male courtesans had set out our treats on a table in the shade of the courtyard. I slid gratefully onto the cool stone bench and poured myself a glass of juice. My mouth was so dry it was sore.

Jenji sat across from me and took a single slice of pineapple. She was thinner today. I wondered when she'd last eaten. I heard that your appetite changed when you evolved.

None of the courtesans ate at all anymore. Nor did they sweat, despite the heat. Only me and Jenji were still defaults; everyone else in the villa had evolved. And now Jenji was evolving, leaving me alone.

"Does it feel weird?" I asked, swallowing a mouthful of cactus juice. Jenji licked her fingers.

"A little. Just sort of numb. Like, I don't know if it's hot out or if I should be hungry or have to pee." We both giggled. "Is it? Hot, I mean."

I thought my sweaty face answered her question. "Really hot. I think I got a sunburn, too."

I had a hard time reading Jenji's face. That was another thing with people who evolved. Their faces didn't work the same way. I could never tell how my mother was feeling.

"I don't think I get sunburned," Jenji said, staring at her hands. Her forehead scrunched up. "I don't remember what it feels like."

I sat back, my sunburned skin tight and aching. I wondered what it must be like, to not feel any of that. It must be like a dream.

Over the next week, Jenji changed. She stopped wearing a hat when we went out into the desert to play. She didn't eat at all, and she seemed to forget how to smile. She evolved faster than I thought she would. It had taken a long time with the courtesans, especially the male ones. I asked my mother about it.

"Men have more trouble evolving, Shi," she said, her gaze not quite focusing on me, despite the fact that I was standing right in front of her. "They have too many emotions, and their bodies feel so much. Because of this they make excellent courtesans, but are very difficult to change."

I sat on the dusty floor, staring at my feet. "I don't want to evolve," I said.

My mother looked towards me—not at me, but almost. "Why not? You will no longer need so many things."

I thought about cactus juice and playing with Jenji. She had started to lose interest in our games. Yesterday, she'd forgotten the taste of pineapple.

"But Ma, you forget!"

My mother's smooth face crinkled. She ran a finger over her smooth lips. Mine were chapped. Faha said I would use up all the water we had, if I didn't evolve soon. I didn't want to go thirsty. I imagined my whole body going chapped, flaking away into the sand.

"What do you forget, child?"

I looked at her. Every day, she looked less familiar. Her body was thin, the linen shroud hanging from her like a pillowcase pegged out to dry. I could count the bones in her hands through her skin when she touched me.

"What's my name?" I asked.

My mother stared at a point just above my head. She sighed. "I'm sorry. I can't remember right now. Ask me tomorrow."

Jenji didn't want to come out and play. I stood in the doorway, licking my lips. "Don't you remember how much fun it is?"

Jenji tied her silk robe closed. The tie pinched her waist so small. Had she always been so much thinner than me?

"I'm sorry, Shi. I don't think you should go out in the desert. It's safer here. And Faha says you're using up all the water."

"I'm the only one who needs it!" I cried.

Jenji looked at me. She was so smooth and so calm. I wondered if there was anything I could say that would make her angry. Or happy.

"It's late," Jenji said. "Why don't you go to bed? Don't you need to sleep?"

"Don't you?" I asked, trembling. She shook her head, no expression creasing her skin.

"I don't know. I don't think so."

When she met my eyes, there was something missing. Something of Jenji gone. Forgotten.

I ran back across the courtyard, the sun-heated rock burning against the soles of my feet.

I sat on my bed with my arms around my legs. Was it so bad staying default? I knew there wasn't a lot out here, but my mother could send for more, couldn't she?

I thought about the last time we had a delivery of food and fresh water. How long had it been? Months, at least. I remembered a time when the deliveries from the city came weekly. Maybe we weren't the only ones running out.

Something bad happened in the city. We moved here to escape it.

I wondered if my mother remembered why.

Out here, there was nothing but dust and the sun. People had to evolve to survive. It started with the courtesans. Then my mother, then Jenji.

Would another delivery come? What if it didn't?

I thought about what I'd do by myself, the only person in the villa who refused to evolve. Faha said that staying default was what killed the land around us. Too many mouths to feed, always hungry and thirsty. The land just couldn't support everyone. We had to evolve to survive.

Before my mother evolved, she said the process was reversible. That when the land recovered and we could grow food again, when there was fresh water and not the tins that we used now—that were running out now—doctors would give everyone a drug to return to normal. We could be defaults again.

I worried that Ma had forgotten this, too.

As the searing heat of the desert beamed through the open window, I pulled all my books off of the shelf. I laid them out on my bed, books about plants that were extinct, books about animals that lived far away. Books about history and stories my mother used to tell me, before she forgot.

When all the books were arranged from biggest to smallest, I opened the drawer next to my bed and took out a pen. I flopped on my stomach and pulled the first book towards me. Its cover cracked when I opened it. The desert made everything crack.

Gripping my pen so hard my knuckles gleamed through my sunburn, I wrote along the blank spaces next to the book's words, putting down everything I could think of. The rules of the games Jenji and I played. The way cactus juice tasted, the sound of the can opener as Faha cranked it along the top of a can of pineapple. The feeling of sun on my neck, and the ache of sunburn. The relief of cold aloe on the burns. The cracking of chapped lips when I forgot and smiled.

I wrote down everything. My memories of Ma, of Faha, of all the courtesans. My earliest memory of leaving the city, smoke in the air and people yelling around us. Maybe there were other villas in the desert, full of defaults evolving one by one. I wrote about the first time I glimpsed the golden sands that surrounded us, about the way evolved people smelled—like dust and leather—and my conversation with Jenji today.

I filled the pages of all the books, from animals to plants to people and back. When I ran out of space and my pen was almost out of ink, I put the books back onto their shelves. With the last ink left in the pen, I wrote on my pillow: B O O K S.

That night I went to my mother. She was sitting in her chair, staring outside. Her hair was a knot on her head, her skin waxy like polished shoes. She looked like one of those mummies in a book Jenji showed me.

I should have written in her books, too. It was too late now. If I went to her to ask, I was afraid she wouldn't know who I was.

"Ma?"

My mother shifted slightly. Her hair crackled against the chair's upholstery. "Shi. My child."

I smiled at my name, then winced as my lips cracked. "I'm ready. To... to evolve."

Ma nodded. She waved her hand, and a male courtesan walked up to me. He was very, very thin. I thought I could count his teeth through his lips. He knelt beside me and held out a syringe.

I wanted to flinch away, but then I thought about the little pile of tins Faha showed me. If I stayed default, there wouldn't be any left for when the doctors came. When they changed us back.

"This will pinch," the courtesan said. I nodded. I knew how it felt. Jenji told me, before she forgot.

The courtesan injected my arm. I felt hot—the desert sun in my veins—and then nothing.

"The First Step in Our Evolution" originally appeared in *Voyage* on 4 August 2020.

About the author

Marisca Pichette is a queer author of speculative fiction, nonfiction, and poetry. Her work has appeared in *PseudoPod, Daily Science Fiction, Room*, and *Apparition Lit*, among others. She lives in Western Massachusetts.

@MariscaPichette

The Skin of Aquila Cadens

Chris Panatier

TRANSMISSION T+10968.0 Authenticate: M. Saenz, Research Barque *Lyrae*

Pod is down from the *Lyrae*, upright and undamaged. Aquila Cadens, population: one. Surface scans show polymorphs of calcium carbonate with intergrowths of dolomite and huntite, limestone. Visual identification of a large iron deposit near the water to the East. No apparent vegetation. No apparent life, unfortunately, but I have only surveyed megascopically. I will put soil samples under glass tomorrow, hopefully. I'll move on to the water after that. See what swims.

Maricella dispatched the message. It wouldn't reach home for twenty-five years. She'd be eighty-nine by then, having long since completed her mission and quit the planet. She leaned over to flip down a row of switches and caught a glimpse of herself in the pod's display screen. The woman that reflected back had been young when she'd set out from Earth almost eleven thousand days ago. She raised an eyebrow and sighed. Half of her life spent transecting the void.

She sealed her helmet and crawled from the pod to stand on the bleached and crumbling caliche-like surface. Aquila Cadens orbited on the outer edge of Vega's habitable zone, but the star was a big girl and could cook dirt just as well as the Sun over desert. The planet's tilt was to the black, meaning it was something like spring at the landing site. Near the end of the mission, going outside would be impossible with the heat, especially in an environment suit.

Maricella instructed the pod to deploy the habitat, though it was more lab than living quarters—a lab-itat. She scanned the horizon as the structure unfolded. The desolate setting aside, the planet had air, water, and the basic elements needed to build life, all facts she and her team had already gleaned through a few inches of glass from light-years away. But the distance muddied the answer to the larger question. For that, they had to see for themselves. The short scan she'd done on her deceleration burn and orbital period hadn't flagged anything. Now, standing on the surface, she was still strangely hopeful despite the subtrace odds.

The little bugs Maricella and her team had developed were an evolutionary grade of mostly free-living protozoans, genetically engineered to concentrate all of the best adaptive and proliferative characteristics. Designed to survive in a wide range of settings, a thousand varieties had been dispatched to potentially habitable planets in the hope that some might stick and jumpstart ecosystems. The Earth—the place it had become—wasn't going to give humankind the time, the decades upon decades, needed for probes to reach planets light-years distant and then beam back their findings. Out of necessity, they'd eschewed a systematic approach, opting instead to fire a shotgun, as it were.

In the runup to launch, her team had worked tirelessly to develop the tiny animals for their brutal charge. Maricella had been consumed by the task, eschewing relationships, pushing friends and family aside in her dogged effort to develop Earth's first world builders. *There'll be time for all that later*, she'd thought. But then came the opportunity to walk upon one of the planets she'd seeded. The trade was thirty years in transit—a no-brainer. She'd leapt at it. Her team had identified eight candidate planets and then drawn lots to decide who would go where. She had gotten Aquila Cadens, a tan-blue marble of desert and sea. It came with an option at the end of the mission to visit another planet orbiting Altair, a nearby main sequence star similar to the Sun.

Four years after sending the bugs on their way, Maricella had set sail.

The bugs were chiefly mixotrophs, able to derive energy both from the consumption of other organisms and found chemicals, or through the photosynthesis of sunlight. The largest group would perform so-called 'soft' terraforming tasks—soil building, water and air purification, consumption of bacteria or fungal pathogens toxic to human life. A smaller subset included those that would occupy native hosts and modify them.

The decision to dispatch bugs that had the potential to permanently alter life on remote planets hadn't come without its share of infighting. The plan was to find life and appropriate it—to enslave a microbial ecosystem in order to serve the purposes of humankind. At the very least, they would be eliminating the ability of native life to freely evolve. But if they were successful, if they actually created something *new*, it would mean they had eliminated what life *had been*—an outcome some of the scientists went so far as to term 'microgenocide'. They'd bickered at length over the ethical considerations, but at the end of the day, the goal was to save the human race. And if it's us versus them, well...

The whole endeavor was contingent on the panspermia hypothesis of life proliferation being correct —that life in the local area of the galaxy shared a common source. If alien genetics were governed by something other than DNA, their bugs would be impotent to carry out their charge, and any philosophical misgivings would remain academic.

The mission allowed just over one Earth-year for surveys and analysis before she had to be up and away. At that time she'd have a choice: aim for home or Altair. The *Lyrae* was fast, but making either destination was dependent on a lone slingshot opportunity with Vega that came in four hundred days' time. Miss that window and she'd be the first human to die on Aquila Cadens.

With the labitat expanded and filling with atmosphere, she grabbed a collection kit from an outer compartment and headed east to where a range of rippling dunes signaled the sea's boundary.

The distance to the shore—only about a thousand meters—felt double in her suit. She hoped it was more the gravity and heat and less the effects of age. In her head she was still thirty-four. At the foot of a large dune, she stopped to catch her breath and hydrate, then took the ascent deliberately, pacing herself to make it up in one steady go.

From north to south, the sea was red. Maricella coughed out a laugh, felt her eyes tearing at the sight. Ignoring her exhaustion, she strode down the face of the dune, falling onto her rear and sliding to the bottom. She dusted herself off and took account.

From orbit it had looked no different than the iron-rich dirt covering huge swaths of ground back home. But she'd been wrong. It was an algal bloom; a red tide. The result, no doubt, of the modified dinoflagellates they'd sent down years before. She trotted to where the gentle surf softened the ground. The bloom meant that the water was packed with phosphorus and nitrogen. So much so that the protists were overeating. Spread out before her was undeniable proof that Earth-based lifeforms could flourish in alien waters. That alone was groundbreaking; fodder for a hundred peer-reviewed papers.

But the floating burgundy cloud was also something else. A telltale sign that the sea was devoid of other DNA-based lifeforms. The algal protists were endosymbionts, programmed to enter the cells of a host plant or animal, graft on the code Maricella and her colleagues had selected, and replicate with the newly revised genome. All in order to incite species diversification and proliferation. The goal had been to create Earth-like analogs in both flora and fauna, riding on the backs of native species. Evolution fired out of a cannon. The fact their symbionts had coagulated into a giant flotilla of algae meant they'd found no hosts.

Maricella stepped into the water until it came to her knees. Viscous, it resisted her movements, so plentiful had her protists become. She couldn't help but smile. It wasn't just the satisfaction that they'd successfully seeded another planet. Their tiny bugs had survived a journey of twenty-five light-years and were thriving, robust. She felt a mother's pride.

She filled several columns with the fecund water and headed back to the labitat. Buoyed by the discovery of her flourishing creation, she floated over the dune and the scorched white caliche.

All night she analyzed the eukaryotes under the scope. It brought another discovery, that not just one species, but several dozen distinct classifications had survived and adapted to Aquila Cadens' brackish water and cloying air. She spoke her findings aloud just to hear a real human voice, lavishing encouragement and praise upon them as she catalogued, even going so far as to name the various subtypes. Desmarella, Rhoda, Aurelia, Gyro, Dino.

TRANSMISSION T+10968.37 Authenticate: M. Saenz, Research Barque *Lyrae*

Happy to report with congratulations to all involved that our little ones are thriving. To date I have counted seventy-nine classifications overall, sixty-one eukaryotes in the local water and eighteen prokaryotes/archaea in ground fissures. No native life identified thus far. All details and data in the upload. I'll be continuing my exploration and analysis moving forward, with periodic check-ins.

Over the coming weeks, Maricella explored tirelessly, consumed by the chance of discovery. Her compulsion, she supposed, wasn't so different from a gold prospector's impulse to keep shoveling. Each new turn of dirt, like each new sample, brought with it a rush of possibilities, the chance to cry *Eureka!*

Every morning she set out in a different direction, stretching the radius of her known world. To the East, the sea. To the North, South, and West, blanched ground veined with cracks that seemed mantle deep. She took samples at varying intervals and depths, plotting the locations so any patterns might later be sussed. Aquila's giant moon was a constant companion, moving ever so slowly through the sky, following along like a milky eyeball. The pod's drones flew sorties out over hundreds of kilometers without noting anything different from what Maricella had seen on foot. Aside from the life they'd sown, there was nothing.

The bugs, though, had done their jobs. Those meant for the soil, a category of archaic diazotrophs, had propagated at around one meter deep, fixing nitrogenous compounds into ammonia, erecting a tentative microbial ecosystem. The waters teemed, swollen and virile, prepared to build new life upon old. But Aquila Cadens was inviolably barren. The rush of discovery from her first day faded, only to be replaced by tooth-clenching frustration. Repeated findings showed the planet and its new denizens in stasis. A holding pattern. Purgatory, in evolutionary terms.

Halfway through the mission, the days became warmer, which meant less time in the field and more in the labitat. When not conducting new analyses or re-running old samples, Maricella allowed her mind to unfold on how life could explode if given but a nudge. The planet was loaded with the necessary elements: oxygen, carbon, hydrogen, nitrogen, and sulfur. Even a modest population of multicellular natives would have allowed her brood to work wonders. She could accept her lot—that a decades-long endeavor would ultimately be fruitless—that had been part of the risk. But her heart ached for the beings they'd created, set forth on winds of scientific optimism, only to end up languishing on the surface of an otherwise dead planet. So much potential wasted.

With the hot season setting in, she could only bear to be outside the labitat in the early mornings and at starset. One evening, as Vega fell in the East, Maricella suited up and headed to the shore where she paced the water's edge. She sang songs. Lullabies she might have sung to a child, perhaps, but now to an audience of countless members. Her red tide. The children of Aquila Cadens.

This became routine. A way to commune with the living that wasn't a recorded transmission twenty-five years stale. Some evenings she carried her melodies into the sea and drifted among the swimmers, gazing skyward as the stars kindled. Together, they devised their own constellations. Something they could share, unique to them and no one else. The Warbler, Saloon Dragon, Sea Fox, Dalmatian Cat... She spoke to them about her life and how, even knowing the outcome, she would do it all over again.

Back in the labitat, Maricella ad-libbed. She ran off-book experiments in the hope of triggering uplift changes in her dutiful spawn, but their fundamental natures were hardwired. The bugs were piggy backers. Absent something to latch onto, they weren't going to elevate. And that was that.

TRANSMISSION T+10968.246 Authenticate: M. Saenz, Research Barque *Lyrae*

One hundred and fifty-four days remaining and there is nothing more to be done. Findings are archived and uploaded. Everything we needed was here, except for the ladder. I will await sling shot and advise of my decision to return home or carry forward to Altair at that time.

Maricella speaks to the bugs, the different varietals. Sings to them. Feels they will understand if she chooses her words carefully, intones her voice sincerely. Carries them about the labitat so they may enjoy changing views and exposures. Her evening floats drag on for hours, so as to be closer to them for longer. She shares secrets. Confesses to them her regret. Whispers apologies. Arrives back at the labitat, her suit's oxygen supply further into the red each night.

One evening, she spills through the pod's hatch euphoric with hypoxia, gathers up the vials for Desmarella, Dino, and Aurelia. Drunkenly, she sways to a song with no name, no melody, rearranges colonies about the lab, perceives the tumble of glassware. Cuts her finger on a petri dish.

The next day, Maricella wakes. Oxygenated, rested. Notes that sobriety brings no relief from the anxiety of coming separation. Abandonment. She pushes up from the floor. On the lab bench is a small tree, red and glistening.

Her little dribble of blood, full of living things. Already co-opted by Desmarella, who has built a delicate bronchus trunk spiked with tiny bronchiole branches. Alveolar buds would surely be visible were Maricella to place a cutting between glass. Given so little to work with, the bugs flex their potential. *Let us show you*, they say. *Oh, what you could have become*, she answers.

Later, silent, she packs her scopes and labware. Places sample columns and vials into cryo for transport, heart crumbling for those she must leave.

In the days leading up to departure, she prepares the pod, clears dust and debris from intakes. The heat, a combination of seasonal change and proximity to the star, is almost unbearable in the suit. She retreats inside, stinking, sweat pooled in every fold, the fingertips of her gloves.

She brings the reactor on-line. Follows protocols. Checklists and calibrations. T-minus fourteen hours.

Night falls to cool relief. She calms, dresses for her swim. The red tide greets her, a bath of her progeny. It is the last evening—she has not concealed the truth. They understand, hold no grudge. And this makes the idea of leaving them unbearable. She wishes them capable of resentment. Hatred at her desertion. Instead, they speak of understanding. Maricella cries until her eyes run dry.

An oxygen alarm pings. She considers letting it go. Even now, the dune is a formidable obstacle for what air she has left. Dying there with her 'zoa, supported on a bed of their flagellae, their tiny hands…she could think of worse deaths. Still, the mission, the future of humankind. She sits upright on the foot of a shoal, her bottom half submerged. Looks to the dune, imagines the ship on the other side, the void, Altair and the Earth beyond that. It is time.

Dawn comes and Maricella is in the water again, murmuring apologies and lamentations. Her mind replays the ethical debates of decades before. Thoughts drift to the cellular phenomenon of apoptosis, where sick cells, such as those with cancerous changes, undergo programmed death so as not to pass on the mutation. And how tumors result when some cells, for whatever reason, refuse to die. She leaves the water and marches back to the pod.

For the first time in four hundred days, she assumes her seat at the controls, brings up the trajectory display. An image of the planet moves in an arc at the end of Vega's invisible tether and two paths emerge. One to a rock in the habitable zone of Altair, and another, to Earth. The countdown begins in her ears, quietly, like a secret. Less than a minute to go. She does not strap in.

As the seconds expire, she considers the blue veins snaking over the bones at the backs of her hands. *Forty seconds.* Their stark topographical relief reminds her that while her body is sixty-four, she's only really lived for just over thirty. *Twenty-five seconds.* She glances at her helmet, hanging nearby. *Ten seconds. Five seconds.* Some cells refuse to die. *One second.*

The panel lights up. Alarms sound. A switch beckons from beneath its plastic guard. Maricella gazes back to the screen and watches until the display re-renders the *Lyrae's* trajectory, and it swings wide of both Altair and Earth. Dotted lines flash from white to red. Apoptosis.

TRANSMISSION   T+10968.400   Authenticate: M. Saenz, Research Barque *Lyrae*

I have chosen not to leave Aquila Cadens in order to pursue a new line of research here. This is my final transmission.

I made you. But I did not give you what you needed to do the thing I designed you to do, my children, my issue. You needed life, and so I give it to you. I give you everything. The future. I give you Aquila Cadens. Make of it what you will.

Maricella selects a panel of her most aggressive endosymbionts and places them into solutions containing her own skin cells, plasma, and cheek swabs. Bulk elements are introduced. Within hours, new structures are visible, stretching and retracting in response to stimuli, respiring. She carries two dishes from the pod, one for the sea, one for the ground.

Mother absorbs into child. She feels the bugs, her sons and daughters, her sexless archaea, drinking in the new information and carrying it into nuclei and organelles. Repurposing. She senses the sharp angle of evolutionary inflection, the moment of speciation, the refraction of static paths, now jagged and ever changing. Nature freed to run wild, each mitosis an exponential leap.

Purple veins crawl like roots through prokaryotic nurseries in caliche crevices. Decided by some combination of eukaryotic programming and terroir, saplings sprout without rain, fleshy pink with thick tufts of autotrophic leaves for capturing Vega's light. All-seeing catkins loll from branches. Elsewhere, bulbs burst skyward with petals that explode in clouds of pastel seed and spore that flow across the planet and take root wherever landed. Maricella, gloves off, reaches down. A threadlike root unspools from a crack and spirals around her fingertip. Communion. She feels the cool depths that the archaea enjoy.

Years pass. Maricella grows old within a failing pod that can no longer clean the air or recycle waste. Outside, she is surrounded by the nascent world her children make. She almost abandoned them once. She would not do it now. She prepares aliquots of Desmarella, Gyro, Dino, Aurelia, Rhoda, and others. Introduces them via nasal mist. Children absorb into mother.

Her body given over, they draft their plans upon her substrate. Endosymbionts take to her cells, slicing in and occupying, editing. They weave and sew filaments of neural tissue into harmony with their primitive structures. Sentience shared, their plans are heard, repeated and circular, aspiring upward. Rung by rung they ascend. Maricella's genome evolves even as she lives. Bound together with her offspring, they become the next thing.

Eureka.

Her mind expands into a network of square kilometers below the planet's surface, aware of all each stripling perceives. Helmetless and fluid, Maricella leaves the pod for good, and is absorbed into the living superstructure that crawls to the horizon. The air, once acrid, is sweet and honeysuckle.

Her children bow and stretch, actualize. They feel pleasure and fulfillment of purpose. She feels it with them. They are a consciousness, the implanted code of primordial lifeforms towering from the human scaffolding upon which they build. A new organism is set on a course of its own making, freelancing within the dictates of the planet's offerings. Maricella's body spills into the network her bugs have created, consumed as raw material; the individual gutters to equilibrium.

The red tide recedes.

"The Skin of Aquila Cadens" originally appeared in *Metaphorosis* on 4 December 2020.

About the author

Chris lives in Dallas, Texas, with his wife, daughter, and a fluctuating herd of animals resembling dogs (one is almost certainly a goat). He writes short stories and novels, "plays" the drums, and draws album covers for metal bands. As a lawyer, he goes after companies that poison people.

www.chrispanatier.com, @chrisjpanatier

Everything but the Moon

Bo Balder

A bell rang through the ship, signaling that the rendezvous with the aliens was half an hour away. The ambassador sat on her toilet and stared at the wall opposite. She asked the toilet to read her the findings again.

"Pregnant, two weeks," it said in its modest I'm-just-an-appliance voice. "Would you like to know the due date?"

All Belkis could think was, *Not now!*

But she had no time to reflect. She pulled her clothes straight and hurried to the ship's gym to join the other ambassadors.

Twenty minutes later Belkis rose on tiptoes to get a better view of the approaching alien vessel. What would they look like? Would those ships really be the future home of humanity?

The ambassadors had been herded into the gym, the shuttle's largest space, to keep the airlock free for the aliens and the military personnel. In space there were no high heels, and Belkis missed them as she peered over the shoulders of taller people.

She'd been a teenager when the Katabiotic aliens tore a path of unreality through the solar system and Earth. Earth was now a dangerous unreliable ruin because of the Katabiotics. Not even the full might of human manufacturing capacity was able to build enough spaceships fast enough to evacuate eight billion human beings. And even if it had been possible, Belkis knew that living on asteroids and stations and clouds of rickety little spaceships was untenable for longer stretches of time. People waited months or years for a turn in a bigger spaceship, where they could breathe clean air and walk around and try to find their families again. That was no life.

Right now humans were begging to buy or trade alien ships from the aliens known as the Gukke. Gukke and human representatives had met and discussed the terms of purchase for these ships. One of these terms had been that the alien ship would choose its own ambassador.

Most of the ambassadors were in their thirties. Old enough to have gained some traction in their careers, young enough to withstand the physical hardship of space-training and the potential dangers.

Belkis shifted her balance to catch a glimpse of the alien ship over someone's shoulder. The ship waved and undulated like a piece of undersea life, a pink and purple sea anemone maybe. Or a particularly fast-growing coral. Seaweed. It was estimated to be over ten kilometers long.

It seemed unimaginable they would dock in it? At it? On it? In only a short time.

A shudder wracked the shuttle. Belkis' stomach dropped, and she clapped a hand before her mouth. Pregnant, oh my god she was pregnant. Although she and Jamie absolutely wanted to have kids, now was not the right time. But at the wild goodbye party on Asteroid Simone de Beauvoir two weeks ago, they'd had been too drunk to think about taking precautions.

The captain's voice calmly said that the shuttle had entered the distortion field around the alien ship. Alien creature. Somewhere on the *Michelle Obama*, UN navy Thruster Class, a bevy of scientists was devouring the data stream and having mental climaxes from nerdy joy.

A dark spot appeared on the side of the alien ship. It grew into a pimple. Or, given its size, a giant carbuncle. A volcanic eruption of ship skin. The carbuncle burst and something reddish and glistening pulsed out. Belkis looked away for a moment to regain control of herself.

A wet thud and a rasping, slithering sound announced the meeting of the *Obama*'s airlock with the alien tube.

"Seal achieved," the captain's voice boomed.

Belkis had gained small spacecraft experience as an SPI investigator on Jacinda Ardern space station a few years back. It seemed like an excellent idea to take position near the exit, where she knew an emergency space suit rack to be located. The aliens had insisted they would provide a safe-for-humans atmosphere. Belkis wanted to believe that, but it always paid to be careful.

The *Obama*'s airlock sphinctered open. A jitter went through the massed ambassadors. People coughed.

The intercom crackled. "The Gukke translator will enter the gym. It has asked that the ambassadors approach one by one and it will pick the lucky winner. I will now transmit the translators' words."

"Shared air. Much newness. Will choose."

It wasn't grammatical Mandarin, but it made enough sense as welcome words.

A midshipman stationed beside her suddenly sprinted away. The alien must be about to enter. The ambassadors ebbed away from the door. Ambitious earth men and women teetered between the instinct to run far away from the scary alien and the desire to be the chosen ambassador. Belkis held on to her position.

A waft of fetid air puffed into the hall. The alien that entered was dark green, larger and squatter than a human, with very short legs and curved toes like an eagle. It seemed to have two pairs of folded arms, or maybe wings? Belkis couldn't see. It had no face.

What did it speak with? Nothing visibly moved on its top bulge, but things wriggled and twitched around the alien's "knees". Human scientists had speculated these smaller aliens were either children, a client species or symbionts. It was unclear if they were intelligent or not.

The candidate who'd ended up at the front stepped out to the alien. One of the smaller aliens shifted from green into a startling blue and wrapped itself around the man's legs. Roberts his name was, or maybe Jones. He had one of those forgettable white-bread faces.

"What do I do?" Jones or Roberts asked, even paler in the face now.

The blue alien turned grey and uncoiled from Roberts' legs. "Confirm: male sex? No egg?" it said.

A sense of giggly embarrassment descended on the group. How did the aliens know about human sexes? Why did they care?

"Male humans?" the translator's eerie, gobbling voice boomed over the intercom. "Become incorporeal."

Belkis kept her amusement to herself.

The male ambassadors protested. The captain confirmed the alien's request. "I confirm: ambassadors of the male sex, please leave the mess hall and report to me."

One of the men stayed. Belkis threw him a questioning look. The ambassador lifted his chin. "They said sex, not gender."

His choice.

The remaining ambassadors trooped forward. Belkis forced herself to leave her station near the emergency suits. She was fully dressed, warm, wearing comfortable shoes, but still she felt naked and unprotected in the presence of the aliens.

As she moved closer, Belkis saw the alien was standing on a kind of platform. The air above it shimmered. A portable air regulator of some kind? One of the smaller aliens doused the translator in a slimy substance. Probably a way to protect it against the human atmosphere. The smell was eye-wateringly awful.

The platform extruded a small limb and scratched itself.

A bio-engineered air regulator? Or a slave species?

Something about the living or semi-living creatures swarming around the translator's feet made her uncomfortable. Note to self: she'd better get used to them in case she was chosen. In fact, this was a good moment to get in front. She managed to slide into second place behind the Han ambassador, earning herself hisses and death stares from other female candidates.

Hey, that was what everybody was here for, right? To get the job. In the SBI dive and space teams she'd learned the hard way about getting the good assignments and promotions.

The testing symbiont embraced the Han Ambassador's knees, turned pink and divested itself. "Follow," the translator said over the intercom. Even this close, Belkis couldn't guess how it made the sounds.

Belkis stepped forward. The miasma of smelly particles roiling around the alien intensified. Her eyes filmed, and her balance seemed to go away, making her float just inches above the floor. She blinked and looked down. Her feet were still there, firmly planted on the deck. The blue alien turned white. She braced herself. This was no time to faint.

The symbiont detached, and she thudded back down in her normal body sense. Whew. That had been strange and unpleasant. Maybe it wouldn't be so bad if she didn't get the job. Aliens and strange chemicals didn't seem such a great mix with impeding motherhood all of a sudden.

"Wait," the translator intoned.

That was a good sign. If you still wanted the job. Belkis breathed through her mouth and watched the other female ambassadors being tested. The symbiont turned pink with each and every one. As the last one trudged dejectedly off, to be debriefed by the captain, Belkis tried to calm herself. This was it. She was going to get the position. Somewhere in the next weeks, after a period of preparation and briefing, she'd be negotiating with the aliens for the lease of a fleet of spaceships. She rubbed her hands, trying to warm them. This was really happening.

Military personnel poured into the gym. A senior officer, she thought the xenologist, rushed towards her. "The airlock, ambassador. Walk with me. We need to talk!"

"Sure," Belkis said. Nobody was congratulating her. Had she misunderstood?

"The alien chose me, right? Can you confirm that for me?" Suddenly it all seemed unreal, as if things had gone on right in front of her that she'd missed.

"Absolutely. You are chosen. Listen, no time to talk about this now. You're it. You've got leave to promise just about everything in the solar system in exchange for the ships, you got that? Except the moon, we need that in case we can return to Earth."

A chill raced down Belkis' spine. She'd boned up about everything Earth had managed to scrounge up that it thought was worthy of interstellar trade. History, geology, art, precious artifacts, DNA databases, bits of asteroids. Trade routes. Whole asteroids. The moons of Jupiter. The planets from Saturn outwards. Nobody had any clue what the aliens wanted.

"What's the hurry? We can talk about this later, yeah? Isn't there going to be some sort of celebration or ceremony?"

The officer shook her head. "You're going right now. They promised us you'd be safe and kept in good health. They brought one of those platforms for you."

The aliens huddled close together on their living platform.

The xenologist grabbed her elbow and seemed to want to drag her over to the alien. Belkis tried to dig her heels in the ungiving polymer of the airlock floor. "What? No. I'm not prepared."

The look in the officer's eyes was a big clue how far these protests would get Belkis.

"I want a spacesuit! A couple of marines to go with me! A gun. Extra air."

"No. We've got to take them at good faith."

Still not quite believing this was happening, the officer gently but inexorably pushed Belkis towards the alien and the undulating tube that connected the space ships. The smell was worse at close quarters.

The xeno officer shook Belkis' elbow. "Get yourself together. You signed on for this."

She walked up to the aliens.

The alien smell intensified. Belkis opened her mouth to make one last demand and an undignified yammer escaped. She snapped her mouth shut. No talking until she could control herself. With that thought she realized how incredibly afraid she was. Jesus. How had it come to this? She'd wanted something like this for so long, had worked so hard for it and now that push came to shove, she was too chicken to enjoy? That just wouldn't do. She could do this.

Being brave was not about feeling no fear at all. It was about being afraid and still doing the job. She straightened her spine and shook the officer's hand from her elbow. She managed to speak without gagging or whimpering. "I'll go under my own steam, thank you very much."

The platform the alien stood on burped, and broke in two. A formless glob of alien stuff fell out of it. It unfolded itself into a small baby platform and stagger around on wobbly legs. The alien air machine had just given birth to a smaller version that was presumably to be hers.

One of the symbionts trotted up to her and held out its manipulator. She had to touch it? With a sense of dread, she put out her hand. She gagged at the feeling of its cool, dry, yet slippery slimy three-fingered manipulator. The sensation was different from anything she'd ever felt. It pulled her towards the baby air machine.

In her head she was already making sense of it. It had to know her, to be able to make air for her. The trembling thing engulfed her hand, briefly, and then turned from a purplish blue to a dark honey hue. The exact color of her skin. How creepy was that?

It must be a DNA reader as well as an atmosphere maker. That was good. She could still use her brain. She could do this.

"I think you should get on the conveyance," the officer said softly in her ear.

The proximity of his voice gave her goosebumps. If she hated anything it was being made to do things not of her own choosing.

"Why so anxious, lieutenant," she said, putting all her bite in her voice while still whispering. "Step away and allow me to do this in a dignified manner. You want it to look good, don't you? Dignified human ambassador?"

The lieutenant gave a painful pinch on her ulnar nerve. "As if we couldn't fix the footage."

"Dignified in front of the Gukke, you idiot," she snapped back.

The officer took a tiny step backward.

That gave Belkis the strength to take one forward.

The newborn air platform wobbled up to her on its stumpy legs and bumped against her shins. Clearly it wanted her to step on it. Beyond it she saw the translator waiting on its own platform, its symbionts clutching the short legs.

They wanted her to go through that flimsy tunnel thing, that looked as if it would sag under her weight and enter the alien ship. Protected only by an alien machine of unproven functionality.

It was just like diving. If your instructor or your buddy said they'd checked your equipment, you had to trust them. You did trust them.

She took a deep breath of safe ship air and stepped onto the platform.

It moved. It was like riding on a roomba, so it must have more than the visible six legs. She could breathe normally, but maybe that was because they were technically still in the airlock. She concentrated on standing centered and relaxed, looking at her feet in their grey printed ship booties. The next time she looked up, she was in the middle of the connecting tube.

She looked back down quickly, but not quick enough not to spot stars through the not nearly opaque enough membrane. She pretended the stars were starfish and she was underwater. Part of her brain insisted on knowing just how deep and provided her with statistics on starfish population per depth. Not helpful. But while she wrestled with memories of snorkeling through coral reefs, a sudden sense of heaviness signaled the entrance to the alien ship.

The quality of the light changed. Belkis realized she hadn't thought about why she had been able to see anything at all in her passage through space. Now she was in a cave-like space, small, rounded, green-lit from below.

The translator stepped off its own air platform and turned towards her. It opened its upper wings partway, showing what was definitely a set of smaller vestigial wings approximately at midriff height. It gestured.

Words sounded. "Please safe. Welcome."

That was reassuring. Ish. Belkis had never felt more alone or less prepared to bargain about the future of the human race. Everything except the moon, check.

She cleared her throat. Even a movement as small as that made her feel dizzy. The platform was less than a foot high and still she had to quash the strong urge to step down and feel solid earth. One, that wasn't solid earth but the internal organ of a giant alien creature, two, that would be suicide. She needed to breathe.

"Please follow me," the Gukke translator said.

Was it her imagination or had it progressed to three-word sentences all of a sudden? And whatever the living air platform did, it wasn't a barrier for sound.

She tried to speak again but choked. Oh my god she was such a failure. She was the fricking ambassador for all of humanity. Get a grip, girl.

"For the citizens of humanity, I am honored to be present on this ship. It is a privilege to meet members of a different civilization. I hope we will be able to communicate successfully towards a happy conclusion of our negotiations."

The translator didn't react.

A dark spot appeared on the far wall, like a bruise or a blemish. It became larger until it burst open with a little belch.

One of the Gukke symbionts ran up to her and threw a dough ball at her feet. That, she could smell. Disgusting. The dough ball grew, split in four, and the four littler balls started growing again. Oh no, she'd gotten her own little symbionts. The smell had dissipated, but it was just gross watching the balls squirm and bulge and produce five knobs. A head and four limbs? Indeed. They turned brown, like her platform, and now she had four little manikins clutching her legs. Her stomach lurched.

Please, let this be all, she silently begged the Gukke. I can't take much more.

As if in response to this, one of them climbed up towards her face. Belkis clapped her other hand over her eyes, wishing she'd never seen the ancient movie Alien and its dozens of remakes.

She, and the drones crawling over her, followed the Gukke translator through the gullet-like tunnel into a huge open space, like the inside of an asteroid. Belkis breathed in with relief.

Another alien, undistinguishable from the translator to Belkis' eyes, started making Gukke speech, presumably not for her benefit. The translator interjected tersely every now and then.

Belkis followed the alien's sweeping wing gestures, taking in the vistas of what the translator assured her would be called Memorial Park. Or Remembrance Fields. Her eyes dutifully dwelled on stands of alien foliage, or maybe internal organs of the gigantic living ship they were standing in.

Whatever it took to stay on good terms with these aliens. Who were either parasites living on the resources of these giant ship-beings, or welcome guests, or lords and masters... translation just wasn't precise enough to convey the meanings of interspecies semantics.

"This ship houses a trillion beings, nearly a billion of my species, but of course there are many creatures great and small needed to make such a vast ecosystem work," the translator whispered in Belkis' ear. The computer aided translation on her screen got no further than "Many beings. Large beings. Small beings. Large being."

How had the translator suddenly started to make so much sense? Had her drones changed her in some way?

She kept her eyes on her alien host, and not on the half dozen small drones that teemed about the alien's large, blue, birdlike feet. They were inconsequential, her host had assured her. Perhaps the host had indulged them a little bit too much. It punctuated this with a slap of its lower wing-arms at a random drone. The lower set were for delicate work, and didn't seem strong enough to inflict much pain. Still.

Belkis would never hit a child of hers. Ever. But then the drones weren't children. Perhaps parasites in their own right, or clones, or slaves, or a separate neutral worker sex like with ants and bees. None of these analogs would match precisely, she knew that, but it was still helpful to try out several. She wanted to understand as much of these aliens and their alien ships as she could.

Her host explained to her that the drones needed to spray her with a special liquid. This was absolutely necessary to mask her presence to the ship. The ship had agreed to receive the human ambassador inside itself, but its mindless host of immune system creatures wasn't under its conscious control.

The drone standing on a pedestal behind Belkis drenched her in a foul-smelling liquid. She closed her eyes just in time. She breathed through it, shocked and dripping. This had to be the worst part.

God, how she longed for a suit. For not to be doused with the anti-immune liquid. For not to smell what she was smelling. Smells were actually tiny molecules entering your nose membranes. What were those molecules doing? They might as well be burrowing right into her cells and changing her DNA, or worse, her baby's.

She suppressed a shiver. So what if she had been chosen from thousands of eager candidates from the diplomatic service because of her track record, her mental stability and relative youth. She was going to tell her bosses it wasn't enough. Nobody could have gauged the effect the sheer presence of so much alien life had on a person. It eroded you from the inside out and the outside in. For all the civility and good nature the translator injected into the alien's words, she was slowly losing it. It was overwhelming. The sights, the smells, the assumptions.

"We're very grateful," she said, careful not to bow her head. The winged aliens looked like predators who liked to swoop down on their prey. A bent neck might kindle all kinds of instincts she would prefer to lie dormant.

"When do you think we can obtain the first ship?"

The alien mantled its wings. The translator offered no interpretation of the gesture. "Right now, dear ambassador, right now! Ship has already created an egg for you, and it's only waiting for the human child to be placed in the incubator with it."

Belkis's hands jerked in an aborted gesture. "What? Why? We asked for a full-grown ship."

"But ambassador, it just doesn't work that way. Ships need to grow themselves to suit each different species. You could not live on this ship for long. It's grown for us, the Fly High."

"How long would it take for the ship to grow big enough?"

"Oh, many revolvings around your sun. But the growth will be exponential for a long, long time. If all goes well, more ships may be created to grow up with humans. But ships don't like to give away their offspring to all and sundry, so we're starting with the one."

Belkis didn't even look at the translation screen anymore. What the translators made from that was magic, and she couldn't imagine warping her brain to be able to do that. You'd have to be a little insane. You would certainly become so over time. Learning an alien language would change your brain. And so would growing up with an alien ship as companion.

"But we didn't know this. And no human parents would give up their child for such an undertaking," she said. "We could donate some skin cells, maybe could you work with that? Or with adult human volunteers?" She would not be on that list for damn sure.

The drone doused her again. A mist of the liquid entered her mouth and made her gag. What had she been thinking, volunteering for this? She already knew why the aliens had chosen her from the final fifty ambassadors. She just didn't want it to be true.

"Those will come on later," the ambassador waved with his middle hands. "The ship needs to be introduced to germ plasma from many different sources if it's to grow and keep a healthy population. But we have to start with one child first, to bond with the ship and guide its growth."

Belkis swallowed and gagged again. "I will tell my government about your demands, but I'm not sure we will be able to meet them. And it won't help us. We need ships that can host existing populations, we don't need to grow new people. We have more than enough of those."

"That is the way ships grow, human ambassador," the alien said. "We can't change that. The ships probably aren't willing to. But you don't need to go back to your human metal ship. The egg is waiting for you."

Her hands jerked again. What were they saying? It conformed her worst fears. She couldn't do that.

The alien said: "That is why we approved of you. You have a child for us."

How did they know? She'd only found out this morning, she hadn't even told Jamie. And she would never ever give her baby away. Even if it only consisted of a few hundred cells right now, or even less? She hadn't even had time to look up pregnancy and its early stages.

Get a grip, she told herself. You need more information before you start panicking. "So are you suggesting that I give up my fetus?"

Belkis was pretty sure she knew the answer. What were her options? She believed the aliens when they said ships had to be grown to suit a species. It made sense. So she and humanity would have to abandon the idea of buying a fleet of ready-made ships completely. That wasn't going to happen. And it sucked, since her people were in dire need right now.

She could in theory just stop the mission right now, return to the *Obama* and report. She'd gained valuable insights about the ships and the Gukke. It wouldn't be a total waste.

If she were allowed to leave at all, that was. She could at least try, or die in the attempt. But that wouldn't make anything better for anyone.

She was completely in the aliens' power. She had no weapons, she was dependent on their technology to return to the *Michelle Obama*. True, the *Oprah Winfrey* and the *Indira Gandhi*, two of the navy's fastest and most powerful pickets were patrolling somewhere near, but was the *Obama*'s captain was prepared to go to war on Belkis' behalf? Maybe. But should she?

She forced herself to think of something besides going to war and losing a child. The future beyond the present need. Look at all the Gukke and their client species, or, who knew, the ship's other inhabitants. What humanity needed was a host of ships that would shelter them. Create living space that was healthy and supportive, and maintainable into a far future, and that was able to run away from Katabiotic attacks.

Would humanity still need the ships in twenty, thirty years? If they survived that long? She bet they would. She had the power to help secure that more distant future. Maybe, and this was a long shot, maybe she could even secure the very best future for her foetus. It would be living on a ship, probably in a major role. It would be safe from the Katabiotics. If he or she found a mate, they might be the Adam and Eve of a new race of space-faring human beings.

"You give the human egg to the ship. Together they will make a ship for humans. You leave," the translator said.

Belkis tried to make up her mind, counting down the moments until the horrible dousing would start again. There was no time pressure. Yet. Eventually she'd get tired and hungry, but that wasn't right now.

At this moment, trading with the Gukke for a future fleet of ships was the only viable deal. It wasn't what she and her people had hoped for, but it was what she could do right now.

This time Belkis didn't stop her hands from interlacing over her stomach. What did her wish for a life with her husband and child mean in the face of this disaster? Not enough. Very little in the face of billions of people's wishes for any kind of life.

"Anything but the Moon," the xenologist officer had said.

An embryo was both more and less than the moon. It was the moon to her and to her marriage, she guessed. Without the child her life would be so much poorer. Maybe she would even break apart, like the Earth, if there was no moon. But wasn't it also a privilege and an honor to give her part of herself up for humankind? Someone would have to do it. If not her, then some other mother. It would be so selfish to let this cup pass away from her.

Salt tears bit into her cheeks and her shoulder shook. How could she even think this? What mother would? What monster would? But how could she not?

She lowered her hands and straightened her spine. Sorry Jamie, she said in her mind. Saying his name made her realize she hadn't named the baby yet. Or told Jamie about it. Sorry baby. Would you be okay with the name "Kai"? I'm going to give you away and I don't even know if I will ever see you again. But I promise to do everything in my power to make that happen.

She looked at the Gukke translator, but no gaze answered hers. They had no eyes.

"I will do it," she said. "Take my baby and raise it with the ship. For humanity."

"Everything But the Moon" originally appeared in *Amazing Stories*
on 4 September 2020.

About the author

Bo lives and works close to Amsterdam. Bo is the first Dutch author to have been published in *F&SF, Clarkesworld, Analog*, and other places. Her sf novel *The Wan* was published by Pink Narcissus Press. When not writing, she knits, reads and gardens, preferably all three at the same time. For more about her work, you can visit her website (www.boukjebalder.nl/bibliography) or find Bo on Facebook (www.facebook.com/bo.balder) or Twitter @bonbalder.

The Firmament

Douglas Anstruther

Guilt is the most relentless emotion. It hollowed out my life and crouched in the shell for forty years. It stayed with me, pointless and unwelcome, even after the Dire Comet wiped away everything that gave it meaning. It didn't matter that no one was left to suffer from what I had done, to judge me or despise me. My guilt remained. The death of my son would pursue me to the ends of the Cosmos.

And what of the Dire Comet? Two years had passed since it came and went. Who was to blame for the sad and untimely death of humanity? As the sole survivor, there was guilt for the taking, but I could carry no more. That burden I left for the Firmament.

I slid from the ornithopter onto aching knees, clutching my dearest possession against my chest. The chaos of the last few minutes still roared in my head, only to be extinguished like a flame between damp fingers when I saw where I'd landed.

I stood on an immense plain of glass — the surface of the lowest Sphere of the Firmament. Stacked invisibly above Earth like concentric layers of an onion, the

Spheres bore the celestial bodies in their paths through the sky. I scanned the distant horizons for the Moon, which this Sphere carried, but saw no sign of it. The air smelled crisp, like ozone with a hint of anise. It was warm and still, in sharp contrast to the icy squall that had just tried to tear us apart and which still raged silently beneath my feet. Far below, bright knuckles of cloud cast shadows over empty viridian forests, and above, the Sun sat, reproachful, in a flawless azure sky.

I walked around the flying machine, looking for a place to set down my bundle. The wrecked ornithopter was splayed across the ground like a bird against a window. The few cloth feathers that had survived the gale formed a halo of debris along with the crystal gear fragments that had been its flesh and blood. Between the mechanical gore and its unnatural posture — in a word, snapped — it was clear it would never fly again.

The glass plain was composed of massive gears the size of city blocks — part of the vast machinery of the Firmament that influenced everything from a person's mood to whether or not a tree fell in a forest. Every second, the ground lurched slightly, which, together with the drifting clouds below, threatened to knock me from my feet. In the distance, the jagged edges of the hole we'd flown through marred the perfect silence with a low, baleful moan. I set my package down and unwrapped its protective blankets, revealing a blue and purple metal box.

"We made it, Zip," I said. "We actually made it to the Firmament." It was hard to believe that less than an hour ago I had filled a pack with food and water, shaved off my hoary beard, combed back my grey hair, put on my Air Brigade uniform with 'Commander Wren' arrogantly emblazoned across the front, and walked out the door of my house.

The box shuddered and came alive. The sides of the box separated, and other plates unfolded from within. Crystalline gears like those of the ornithopter, doubtless harvested from somewhere in the Firmament, whirred beneath. Legs emerged, and after a minute of clicking and buzzing, a mechanical creature, roughly the size and shape of a beagle, stood before me. An elaborate, blue letter T was stamped across his forehead. He shook himself with an unhealthy clanking sound, made a few excited laps around me, then sat on his back haunches and gave me a meaningful stare.

"C'mon now, Zip. You know that I don't ever know what you want." Yet, somehow, he had brought me here. Only a week had passed since I stumbled across this strange creature, rummaging around in my tool shed. In that short span he'd become the entirety of my life, and, I had no doubt, was well on his way to becoming the cause of my death.

He got back up, wagging his tailless back end, and trotted toward the belly of the stolen ornithopter — stolen only inasmuch as it wasn't mine and was used without permission. Technically, it wasn't anyone else's either, since there *was* no one else. In a way, I was the richest man alive, having inherited the Earthly possessions of every single person. And I'd just left it all behind. Aye, that was okay. I couldn't bear another moment alone on that empty world. I wanted to be with Zip, and Zip wanted to be here.

"Right," I said, following after him. "Apparently, I'm taking orders from a mechanical dog now. I had some ridiculous commanders back in the Air Brigade, but at least they were human."

Zip reached the ornithopter's storage compartment, latched onto a handle, and pulled, his little metal feet clanking and sliding ineffectually on the smooth ground.

"Here, let me help you with that, little guy." I reached down and opened the panel, revealing a compartment packed with fabric. Zip and I looked at each other for a moment, then Zip latched his jaws onto the cloth and began pulling, with just as much effect as before.

"Go on, I'll get it. You're just in the way now. Go on, git." He blinked cute puppy-eyes at me but got the message and backed away.

Half an hour later I'd liberated the contents of the compartment and spread it across the ground. At the heart of the fabric, we found a wicker basket filled with cables and struts.

"A hot air balloon?" I asked, eyeing the metal beagle with mock suspicion. "How did you know that was in there?" Zip yawned, ignoring my question. It didn't matter, really. He just knew things. Like he'd known where to find the ornithopter and how to get me into it and up through that hole.

A red hand crank was bolted to the lip of the basket. Zip stared at it with comic intensity, so I took the hint and started cranking. Slithering cables gathered the fabric and lifted it onto struts which rose from the basket. It was slow going and I had to rest often. Meanwhile, Zip zipped around (thus his name) and the world below marched slowly past. The Sun, however, remained fixed in the same spot of the sky, as if nailed there. Eventually, Zip settled down, watching me from above outstretched legs. The hole we'd flown through wandered around to the other side of the 'thopter, carried by the clockwork motion of the ground. I wondered what the great gears were calculating, now that everything they influenced was dead. Everything, but me.

The last item to rise from the basket was a burnished metal tank that positioned itself beneath the fabric aperture. Once this was in position, Zip marched up to the basket, stretched his front legs toward its top, and waited for me to pick him up and set him inside.

"Aye, let's go, then." I said, dropping my pack into the gondola, and hoisting the wiggly creature into the basket. I squatted next to him, beneath a great, two-pronged switch on the tank that was labelled with the word "Lift." I did, and so did we.

It had been two years since the malign red glow of the Dire Comet made its appearance in the southern sky. Half a year later, everyone was dead. Everyone, of course, except for me. They called it the Fate Plague and it brought death to everyone in their own way. It wasn't actually a plague, so much as a curse — a sharp turn in humanity's destiny, straight into a brick wall. Sure, some died from disease, a sudden fever or a scalding rash that came out of nowhere and left the victim dead in a matter of hours. But most people died of freak accidents — train wrecks, air crashes, car accidents. People became terrified to leave their houses, but it didn't matter; a walk across the living room could be just as deadly. No creature was spared, not even the animals. Anything larger than a fruit fly shared humanity's fate, which hardly seemed fair, since everyone knew that humans were the cause. It was humans, after all, that had broken the Firmament. The rest were just innocent bystanders.

For a long time, I was oblivious — too wrapped up in booze and self-pity to notice anything. Later, after it became clear what was happening, I waited my turn at home, resigned to the end of a dreadful life. When the radio went silent, and the lights went dark, curiosity and boredom overcame me and I ventured out. I wandered for weeks, finding nothing but corpses. Eventually, I returned home and waited some more.

The loneliness was as terrible as it was unexpected. Before the Plague, I had no friends, no family, no acquaintances that would check on me or care if I became ill. I lived in a deep rut of my own making that was largely unaffected by the end of the world. I was used to being alone, but this was worse. It was yet another way of not belonging — the ultimate snub, the final rejection. Even in death, I was left out.

Technology had been advancing quickly when the Plague struck. Computers made from components harvested in the Lower Spheres — the ones that carried the Moon, Mercury, and Venus — had been getting better every year. The space between the Upper Spheres — which carried the Sun, Mars, Jupiter, and Saturn — was filled with celestial waters. The waters above the Sun had been powering cars and machinery for half a century. Exotic waters from more distant Spheres were just starting to make it to Earth and promised amazing advances: frictionless railways, personal flight, even floating cities. Weeks before the appearance of the Dire Comet, the papers had been filled with the discovery that the furthest waters, those beyond Saturn, affected the flow of time. What marvels could be achieved when we controlled time itself? But instead, it all came to an end.

I looked down at Zip, curled at my feet in the bottom of the gondola. He was like nothing I'd ever heard of before — a mechanical animal, with thoughts and plans and feelings. The T on his forehead was the symbol of the Tinkers Guild, the most advanced Astrological Scientists and Engineers in the world, but even the Tinkers had never made anything like Zip. Except that it looked like they had.

The green Earth slid beneath us under the perpetual daylight. The Lunar Sphere that we had just left gradually faded away, a trick of light that all Spheres shared, giving the Earth an unimpeded view of the stars, and vice versa. Only the celestial bodies they bore were visible from afar. It had something to do with the angle of light, I recalled. Although I could no longer see the Sphere, I still felt its influence — the barest hint of an emotion I hadn't felt in a long, long time. Happiness.

The adrenaline of the previous day drained away into the calm air and I slumped down into the bottom of the basket, where dream found me. It was a variant of the usual theme. In this one, my son, Sammy, didn't die. He fell into the pool while I was passed out drunk, but somehow was able to get to the edge and crawl out to safety. I was scolded by friends and family for nearly letting the unthinkable happen. I felt terrible, but, in the end, everyone was just happy that Sammy was okay. It would have been a nightmare for anyone else, but for me it was a good dream. There was no messy divorce, no shunning by my family, no being cut off from everyone I knew or loved. I woke up relieved, basking in the warmth of family and friends. Except that a minute after I woke, nothing remained but a painful hope of forgiveness, forever denied.

I stood and stretched my stiffening legs. Zip woke too, and we spent the next few hours goofing around as the balloon rose. He nipped at my fingers and did figure eights between my feet. I told stories I hadn't shared for decades. When I spoke he sat attentively, head slightly cocked, looking at my face. I didn't know if he understood me, but he listened well.

A hazy oval moved across the flawless azure sky. I thought it was a cloud at first, then I remembered the clouds were all far below. It grew closer and larger, as the wind blew us toward it. Suddenly my perspective shifted, and I realized I was looking up at a hole in the Second Sphere, the one that carried Mercury. It was rotating toward us. And quickly.

I had a moment of raw terror as events accelerated beyond my control and we were sucked through the gap like smoke through a cracked window. As we moved above the Second Sphere, the flawless blue into which we had been ascending stayed below, leaving the new sky a stark white that was hard to look at, and giving the surface of the Mercurial Sphere, now below, the color of blue arctic ice. Its features seemed unreal, like blueprint sketches overlaid on the thin air. Far below, through it all, swam Earth, its curved edges and pregnant swell making it look like a great dome beneath an ocean.

"Guess the blue skies end here, Zip."

The balloon struggled to rise against the hot, thin air and we floated lower, skimming the craggy surface. Translucent mountains straddled the distant horizon, dripping cataracts of deep blue that became rivers, lazily wandering across plains toward us. No living thing moved; it was as lifeless as the world I had left — worse, for the absence of plants. Yet something about the translucent terrain gave life to the angles beneath the surface. The intersecting lines gave it a depth and complexity that opaque terrain lacked, and the distant mountains hypnotized me with their inner complexities. It didn't feel barren. It felt alien.

We barely cleared a row of serrated ridges that opened onto a long, serpentine beach. The gondola touched down and tipped over, throwing me on top of Zip. I fumbled around as well as I could, trying to keep my weight off him while the balloon dragged us across the beach, covering us both with blue sand. I was able to crawl out just as the deflating balloon caught a breeze and the entire thing started to lift again, with Zip still inside.

"No!" I stood and leapt, getting my hands on the rim of the rising basket and pulling it down. After a brief wrestling match, I triumphed and pinned it to the ground at an angle where Zip could crawl into my arms. The two of us collapsed to the ground as the balloon took off again toward the strange sea.

I sat up and caught my breath while Zip launched into play. He raced across the sand in great, gleeful bounds, scooping up mouthfuls of sand and spraying them around with a shake of his head. I'd never seen him so happy; it was a delight to watch and some small portion of his carefree joy spread to me like a contagion.

The air carried a faint tinkling sound, like distant windchimes, that gave me terrible *déjà vu*. Beneath me, the translucent blue sand felt strange, like foam padding, and was warm to the touch, with a faint smell of heated metal. Motion within it caught my eye. I patted down my pockets until I found my reading glasses, glad to see they were neither lost nor broken, and used them to examine the sand more closely. Each grain was a tiny transparent gear. The ones I scooped up or disturbed sat motionless, inert, but the ones on the ground turned in lockstep with the grains around them. I moved forward on hands and knees, watching the motion of the sand. In some places the motion of the little gears sped up or slowed down, in others it coordinated to form whirls or streams and in others it was a chaotic mass of motion. The Tinkers had made their first computers from these sands, before switching to more advanced materials from the Venetian Sphere. Again, I wondered what arcane calculations the sands of this beach were making. Was it calculating where lightning would strike? Which stones would break away from cliffs?

The influence of the Spheres had been well known for centuries. Understanding their effects had been the basis of the Scientific Revolution, and materials harvested among them had ushered in the Industrial Revolution that followed. Once the exploitation of the Firmament was underway, specialized sciences had risen, devoted to influencing destiny by changing the topology of the Spheres. If someone needed something to go a particular way, they consulted the charts, then levelled a mountain on this Sphere, or dammed a river on that Sphere, and the chances rose fifty percent, or twenty, or ten. The results had never been foolproof, but they had been known to sway the outcome of lotteries, elections, or even wars. Ultimately, the damage done to the Spheres to feed technology and tweak destiny had led to the Dire Comet.

Some of the distant foothills had a red hue, like a patch of inverted color after looking at a glare, but fixed to the land. Each place with this red hue was disfigured in some way, flattened hills, scarred mountainsides. My footprints bore the same red hue of destruction — faint and barely visible. I watched an area of disrupted sand for a few minutes and saw how the motion of the surrounding grains slowly pushed those I had disturbed back to their original positions and set them spinning again. As the footprint slowly healed, its red tinge faded.

So the Firmament could heal itself. And yet, those distant foothills still glowed red, years after their wounding. I wondered how long it would take for them to heal, if ever. I felt a kinship with these strange realms, still damaged even after the world had ended.

I stood up, stretched my back and worked my way to the water, stiff-legged after crouching for so long. Waves lined the beach, but frozen in time. Light sparkled and moved within the motionless water with a diamond radiance. I leaned over and put a fingertip against the leading edge of a wave, felt a prick and came away with a bright spot of blood.

The nettle water reminded me my own supply had been lost with the errant gondola. The Spheres were famous for their sterile lack of life and now it didn't look like I'd be replenishing my water either. How much longer would this adventure with Zip last? I wasn't afraid to die, but would prefer it not be of thirst.

Zip climbed a small mound of sand that extended beyond the waterline and sniffed the motionless waves cautiously. Suddenly the sand gave way beneath him and he dropped into the water, where he thrashed about, sending out spumes of pink spray. For a second, I thought he was enjoying himself, then I saw panic in his movement. He let out a frightful screech and slipped beneath the surface. I sprinted to the water's edge and dove in.

It was like diving into a sea of needles. I pulled myself down toward where I'd last seen my companion and groped around, desperate to feel anything solid against my flailing arms. Each movement was a caress against splinters. Something brushed the back of my hand. One mighty breaststroke later, I felt his weight crash against my shoulder. I closed my arms around him and kicked up, breaking the surface to the muffled sound of shattering glass. The last thing I remember was collapsing on the shore. My legs were still in the water, but my arms were on the beach and Zip was safe.

Dreams circled me like sharks around a wreck, all of the same malign species. In these, Sammy did not escape the price of my neglect. The unthinkable event that defined my life was thought. Sammy drowned. Because I was too drunk to do any of the simple things that could have prevented it. "No, Sammy, don't climb over that wall." "Sammy, I'm serious, that's dangerous." "I'm coming Sammy!" "Breathe, Sammy, c'mon." "Aye, Sammy, cough it out." "Boy, don't you ever scare me like that again." I never said any of those things. Instead, the dream told me there was a splash. A cry for help that went on, and on, becoming more desperate, then tired, then only silence. Had my mind filled in how it must have happened or had some part of it been listening? Either way, it offered the dream to me, over and over, as the perfect punishment. Not only did I have to watch Sammy die, I had to watch myself, sloppy and disheveled, sweaty and weak, having chosen foul drink over the life of my own five-year-old son, lying inert except for heaving breaths, as my son died.

The familiar dreams of heartbreak and remorse were interspersed with impossible scenes, more fantastic than any dream: sliding beneath the canopy of a blue crystalline forest, lying motionless upon the sky, dangling over the world from an impossible height. At times, a grown Sammy looked down at me with concern. Pain and the blinding glare of daylight were the only constants.

As a child, whenever I was sad or hurt my mother would scoop me up in her arms, take me outside into the cool night air, and reach toward the stars. "Touch a star, baby. It'll make everything better." I'd copy her, straining my little arm up, wanting badly to feel better, to tap into that power. It always worked. But now, night never came. The stars were banished, and I could never get better. The thought of it made me so sad that I started to weep.

"Wren? Why are you crying?"

It took me a long time to realize the significance of the words. Someone was talking. Someone. It was the most impossible hallucination of them all, because there was no one left to speak. I reached my hand to my face to clear the tears and the blinding brightness, but it stopped just before my eyes with the clinking sound of glass against glass.

A few rapid blinks cleared my vision and I found myself lying flat on my back, looking up into the arched interior of a massive crystalline building where rainbows fluttered like bats.

"Are you in pain?" The voice had a strange buzzing quality. *At least the insects survived,* I thought, not quite having escaped the grip of my dreams.

"No," I croaked. "Gone." I wasn't sure if I was correcting myself or answering his question.

"That's good," the voice answered. It sounded kindly, almost familiar. The memory of my adventures with Zip returned like a work of art revealed with the pull of a sheet, and the last residues of sleep fled my brain. I was in the Firmament. Talking to someone. Had this been Zip's plan all along, to reunite me with survivors among the Spheres? A brief moment of excitement at the prospect became a battlefield of competing emotions. Hope for the survival of humanity clashed with anxiety and dread at the thought of having to interact with people. Ultimately, the latter claimed the high ground and couldn't be dislodged.

With effort, I propped myself up onto my elbows, making a clatter that echoed through the vast space. I was lying on a stone slab, surrounded by a knot of retracted machinery. My skin glowed red, like the damaged lands of the Second Sphere, and was covered in a shell of glass, like trees after an ice storm. I shifted myself onto one elbow and brought a hand up in front of me, flexing my fingers into a fist. They were stiff but functional. I strained to sit up further and see the rest of my body.

"I'm sorry. I couldn't save all of you," the voice said.

I wondered whom he couldn't save. Then I looked down, and understood. Beneath my belly button, the denuded skin curved away sharply toward my spine. Below that, there was only glass in the shape of feet, legs, and a groin as smooth as a doll's.

"What ... what happened to me?"

"The lake on the Mercurial Sphere eroded your flesh. I brought you here; the Tinkers' machines did the rest."

Questions crowded my lips. I tore my eyes from my own body to the source of the voice. A humanoid automaton with articulated plates of blue and purple, like some ancient armored warrior, stood by my side. The smooth purple dome of his head framed a single piece of blue ice with the kind eyes and warm smile of a young man. His features moved in a stepwise but otherwise lifelike manner. An elaborate, blue letter T marked the metal above his face.

"Zip?" I asked, dumfounded. "Is that you?"

"Yes, Wren. I'm the same entity that you have been referring to as 'Zip' "

"How ... ? How can that be you?"

"I grew," he said matter-of-factly. "You were too large for me to carry, so I activated an auto-assembly protocol and used raw materials from the Mercurial Sphere to change my form."

"Where are we now?"

"We are in the Great Venetian City, built by the Tinkers."

"Venetian? We're on the Third Sphere?"

"Yes."

"How were you able to get me all the way to the next Sphere?"

"It was difficult. There's a lift at the heart of this city that transports things from a particular mountaintop at particular times." He tilted his head and looked at me, perhaps trying to read my emotions. "We were fortunate to have made it in time."

"Fortunate." I looked down at my legs, and to my astonishment, my right ankle flexed, and then my left; I could move them. I raised a glass leg from the cool slab, swung my hips around, and sat up with surprising ease.

"Amazing," I said.

I stood and took a few steps around with none of the usual stiffness I'd come to expect. Still, I felt broken. Not because part of me was gone, but because I didn't care. It should bother me that I'd lost half of my body. I supposed it was the same morbid indifference to life that I'd carried with me all these years. Add to that my casual acceptance that this journey would result in my death, and it just didn't seem to matter that I was only half a man. Or less.

"The infirmary built replacement legs," Zip explained.

"And what about this?" I asked, holding out my arm, and then touching my face. "This glass coating."

"It's a special Tinker glass. It was infused into your body to repair damaged organs and replace your skin."

The level of technology on Earth prior to the Dire Comet had never been anywhere near this advanced. "It seems the Tinkers had quite a few tricks up their sleeves," I said.

Zip handed me a small pile of clothes he'd found in the city. I dressed myself in the white, loose-fitting garments, among benches of strange equipment and beneath the glare of the engorged sun, which hung unmoving on the other side of the chambers' transparent walls.

"I want to show you the City, Wren. I think you'll like it. But we don't have much time."

"Why?"

"We must keep going."

"Okay, Zip. I think it's about time I started getting some answers. First off, where are we going?"

He looked puzzled, as if he didn't understand why I would ask such a question. "We're going up."

"Yeah, okay, but what is our final destination?"

"All the way."

"All the way. You mean to the Stars?" I asked, incredulous. The celestial waters above the Sun made travel in the Upper Spheres all but impossible. Some surveyors and bold speculators had ventured past Jupiter, but only a handful of the sturdiest explorers had ever made it past Saturn. None had reached the fixed Stars that marked the furthest limits of the Cosmos.

Zip looked as if it was something he hadn't really considered before. "I guess so. I just know we must keep going."

"Why?" I asked.

He smiled broadly, happy at last to have a question he felt comfortable answering. "Because the Tinkers created me to take you there."

"But why? Why did they want me to go there?" I asked, anger rising within me.

Zip wilted at my words. "I'm sorry, Wren. I don't know that."

Seeing how hurt he looked to have upset me drained all my anger. Just because Zip could talk didn't mean I'd get any more answers out of him.

"Aye, Zip. Why don't you go ahead and show me the city, then?"

After the first couple of corners, I was hopelessly lost, but Zip seemed to know his way. We passed from one building to another along winding staircases and towering archways, always going higher. Beautiful, complicated things spun or twisted on their own. I didn't know if they were machinery or art or both. It was a city of towers and far-flung arches that reached for the sky as if grown. Everything was made of the same light-shearing crystal that populated the city with rainbows from the light of the ever-present, over-large Sun. It was a city for celestial beings, if any had bothered to exist.

As we rose, the skyline took the shape of a great onion dome, beyond which a labyrinthine wasteland of jagged, wind-carved crystals reposed in fantastic shapes. Beneath it all, the Earth swam and shimmered, distorted by the city's frenetic angles.

"I remember hearing about this place," I said in a reverent tone. "The Tinkers built it something like forty years ago, then abandoned it ten years later, just when people were really starting to harvest the Spheres. They said —" and then it came to me. "They said we were damaging the Spheres. That everyone needed to leave."

"Yes. I remember that too. Although I did not exist then," Zip said.

"We didn't leave, though," I said sadly.

"No."

He led me to an overlook near the top of the central dome. A central spire rose from the dome, disappearing into the brightness of the white sky.

"That's the way to the Fourth Sphere. The one that carries the Sun," Zip said, pointing at the spire. "When the city was inhabited, passengers and materials moved up and down the spire automatically." He looked at me. "We'll have to climb it."

"Zip. I don't understand. How do you know all this? How did you know where to find that ornithopter? How did you know it would have a balloon in it? How have you gotten us this far?"

"I just know where to be and when. And I know we must keep going. Now."

"That's gonna be a long climb, Zip." I shielded my eyes against the nearby Sun. "And it sorta looks like we'll be climbing right into the Sun." The air was already hot, although the glass coating of my body helped, and sweating seemed to be a thing of the past.

"It will be difficult."

"Aye."

The spire was small enough for the tips of my fingers to touch on the other side if I hugged it. Each side had its own set of rungs with room for one person. I climbed on one side and Zip on the other. After an hour of climbing, the Venetian City and the rest of the Third Sphere were no longer visible beneath us. The spire tapered to invisibility at each end, making it look as if it were floating in the air — a compass needle pointing from Earth to Sun. Below, Earth rotated slowly, its edges dropping away from the horizon in a way that showed its true nature as a sphere. *How far one must come*, I thought, *to see the truth.*

I told stories of growing up on the farm, my days in the Air Brigade, meeting my wife, the birth of our son. I was surprised how many stories I had, how happy they were. There was no hint among them of the dark turn my life would take.

Time passed, but without the motion of the sun, there was only my growing fatigue to mark its passage. At some point I realized that I hadn't become hungry or thirsty since waking up in the Venetian City. It seemed that part of me was gone too. The muscles of my arms burned terribly, but my legs, which were doing most of the work, felt fine. When I could go no further, I locked my legs around a rung and reached my arms around the spire, where Zip held them from the other side. In that strange position I fell immediately into a fitful sleep with dreams of falling like a ragdoll, reversing my spin each time I struck a rung on the way down. In some of these I knocked Zip from the spire as I fell, which always woke me with a start of panic. When I wasn't resting, we climbed.

The sun did move, slowly. It crept toward the zenith and swelled until the spire disappeared into the heart of a vast, bulging lake of fire that crackled overhead and scorched the top of my head and shoulders, even through their protective coating. I squeezed my eyes shut against the brilliance, reaching blindly for the next rung that was always hotter than the last.

The heat and supernatural monotony made me delirious and I climbed in a fugue state. I imagined the Spheres as a vast spinning machine that had conspired to replace my legs so that it could lure me into its great flaming mouth.

Zip moved to the same side and climbed ahead of me to shield me with his shadow. Eventually the heat became so intense that I could do nothing but cower behind my companion and hold on. I lost time. Eventually a breeze, cooler than most, rustled my senses and I saw that the sun had slid past us; the spire no longer shot into its heart but into the blank sky. We clung there a while longer, hours at least, maybe days, to let the sun move further away. It was only a little, but it made all the difference.

"We don't have much time. We have to reach the cross-over before Venus goes into retrograde," Zip shouted over the roar of the Sun.

"Aye," I answered, not understanding a word of it.

"We have to start climbing again."

We continued for another blurry stretch of time, until I reached up for the next rung and found only air. The shock of it nearly sent me tumbling, but I held on. The spire had ended, and we clung at its tip like two ants at the end of a very long blade of grass.

"What now?" I shouted.

"There." Zip pointed away from the sizzling sun. I didn't see anything at first but then another spire emerged, reaching down from the featureless sky. It was identical to the one beneath us and I realized with a jolt of dread, that after all we'd been through, we were only halfway to the next Sphere.

"No. Zip. I can't climb anymore." The spire shot toward us at startling speed; it was either going to crash into us or roar past.

"It's going to be okay, Wren. Just a little further."

The spire slowed. By the time it was close enough to make out individual rungs, it was moving no faster than a brisk walk. It slid gingerly into position above our spire, lining up perfectly, with a gap no wider than the width of a hair between the two, and stopped.

"Now," Zip shouted. "Quickly." He scrambled onto the upper spire. I followed, exhausted and sluggish. A moment later the two spires separated, our new perch heading back in the direction from which it had come.

"I think this one still works," Zip said. He grasped the ladder and squeezed his eyes in concentration. A moment later he was sliding upward, carried by moving rungs.

He stopped and looked down at me. "The Venetian Glass touches every part of you, even your brain. You can use it to control the spire. All you have to do is concentrate."

It wasn't quite as easy as that, but I got the hang of it quickly. It was like imagining yourself scratching an itch that wasn't on your body. I caught up to Zip and shot past, shouting childhood taunts as I did. He overtook me and we continued like that, racing our way upward, until the bottom of the Fourth Sphere loomed into position above.

The Sphere that carried the Sun wasn't solid, like the others, but a lattice of massive crystalline girders. Together, they formed an immense three-dimensional labyrinth. I was surprised, because this was the Sphere that held back the celestial waters. I couldn't remember from grade-school Astrology classes what kept the waters from raining down onto us, but I figured I'd find out, firsthand, soon enough. Zip led us through with confidence, climbing up steep beams with precipitous drops on either side. The sunward side glowed a deep red.

"Almost seems like you've done this before, Zip."

"I have not. I just know the way." He paused before speaking again. "My first memory is waking up in a warehouse. The door was open and I walked straight to you. Like always, I knew where to go, but not why."

"Aye. Like always."

We navigated the dangerous path a while longer before Zip spoke again. "They chose you."

"Beg pardon?"

"The Tinkers. Somehow they manipulated the Spheres to protect you, after the Fate Plague started."

"Why?"

"Because you're special. And when you go up … I don't know. Somehow things will be better."

Special. I couldn't even protect my own son, and for the rest of my life I'd done nothing but drink and suffer. I shook my head. "I'm afraid they're going to be terribly disappointed."

The Solar Sphere was far thicker than the others. We walked along beams that looked like girders placed by giants. The blood-red glow from the sunward side pulsed gently. It felt as if the Cosmos were a giant organism, and that Zip and I were two microbes slinking past its living heart. Eventually, the space became more compact and I had to duck beneath crossbeams. It became slow going as the trusses closed in on us and we were reduced to crawling, first on hands and knees, then on our bellies.

"I can't make myself any smaller, Zip. Something's got to give."

"Just a little further."

Although everything around us continued to grow tighter, narrower, closer, our path began to widen. Someone had carved it out of the surrounding supports. We were nearly able to stand again as we walked through solid crystal, still lit red by the distant sun. The narrow walkway spiraled upward, until it opened onto a small room.

"This is our ride from here." Zip said, pointing to a pod of smooth metal the size of a small car, resting on the floor of the room. A blue Tinker's symbol glowed on its side. Zip placed his palm over the symbol and a panel rose on each side, revealing padded seats within. He motioned for me to take a seat. I looked at the room anew, noticing a seam across the ceiling. The passage we had come from had already irised closed.

"A submarine?" I asked.

"Yes."

"I guess that makes sense." After all I'd seen, it was still hard to imagine that we were just beneath the bottom of a vast celestial ocean. "Onward and upward, eh?"

I sat in the vehicle and Zip got in on the other side. Exterior lights snapped on and the vehicle's walls faded to transparency. There were no controls, but Zip closed his eyes and concentrated, like he had on the spire. The sub's doors closed with a hiss and the seam above us split apart, creating a thin waterfall that became a flood that quickly filled the room. We rose through the opening into a strange black ocean of stars.

The opening fell away quickly and by the time it had closed, the Sphere had already disappeared beneath us, in that peculiar way that all Spheres become invisible with distance. The Earth was now an immense, brightly lit, blue and green ball, floating against a background of stars, more numerous and brighter that I'd seen on the clearest of nights. The Sun, a squat, angry blister of fire, slid away from us, and the roar of its conflagration drained from the interior of the sub as it went. I was glad to see it go; I had had quite enough of the Sun for a while.

The two of us floated serenely up toward the next Sphere. It wasn't long before a deep, dreamless sleep claimed me and held me for what felt like a long time. When I woke, Zip was looking down at the shrinking Earth, now no larger than my outstretched arms.

It occurred to me that we were moving through the same waters that had powered every mechanical device on Earth for decades. A leak and a spark would be enough to engulf our little cabin in flames. There was danger here, and once again, I couldn't bring myself to care. But this time was different. My lack of concern didn't come from self-loathing or a morbid disregard for my life. I had come far and endured a great deal since leaving home. I looked back on my journey and saw that I was no wilting daisy. There was something to be proud of there. And so, within the usual soup of ennui, there was a hint of something I hadn't felt since my time in the Air Brigade — a sense of confidence. It was like finding a cherished object, lost long ago.

"What's next for us, my friend?"

Zip looked at me, tilted his head the way he did when he was reading my expression, and smiled. "I don't know, Wren. More adventures, I imagine."

I smiled, leaned back in my chair, closed my eyes and said, "Aye."

The days passed erratically when measured against my own muddled sense of time. The Sun drifted away, flattening itself into a line and then squeezing itself behind the Earth, which became a round absence of stars, a drain into which starlight disappeared. Meanwhile, ahead, a red star grew brighter and brighter.

"We need to cross the next layer near Mars itself. It's the only place where the path through the labyrinth is known," Zip explained.

Mars was a featureless bulge the size of a large city that glowed a brilliant red. The Sphere that carried it consisted of the same latticework of girders and supports as the one that bore the Sun, but was far thinner, with larger gaps. The Solar Sphere had held back the celestial waters. Here, the waters above Mars floated on the Solar waters like oil above water. Zip navigated the ship through the complicated twists and turns of the lattice and we emerged at the edge of the dark side of Mars.

On this side, Mars was a jet-black disc, sealed beneath a blue transparent dome. A ring of posts around the dome's perimeter bore mirrors that reflected sunlight onto a medieval city of red bricks surrounded by fields of black dirt. I vaguely recalled hearing something about a Mars Colony years ago but had never given it another thought.

Forms moved among the buildings. There were people there!

"Zip, Zip, Zip. Look. People. Living people. We've got to go to them."

A light flared and died away on the far side of the city. It was then that I noticed the buildings were all in tatters, the fields barren. Another light blossomed, closer to us.

"What's happening down there?"

"The Mars Colony has been at war with itself since the Dire Comet appeared — fighting over limited resources. We can't risk them seeing us, Wren. They're dangerous."

"But humanity isn't dead. There's still hope. If there are other people —"

"The colony has no women, no children. It has no hope."

"No, no. I don't believe it. How do you know all this?"

"In the Venetian City there are machines that can see … everywhere. There are only a few dozen men left here, and they will fight until there is nothing left."

"Maybe we can evacuate them down to Earth. Maybe the Tinkers sent us to rescue them."

A group of men spotted us and pointed in our direction as we rose past the dome. One of them typed into a keypad and something near the mirrors swiveled around and lined up with our ship.

"Watch out Zip, I think they're going to —"

Light flared from the turret and our ship rocked.

"Hang on," Zip said. He squeezed his eyes closed and we leapt upward, throwing me back in my seat. The dome shrank away from us while the turret kept barking light, joined by several others.

"I can't believe we're leaving the only people left alive in the Cosmos. Maybe if we came in from below, out of range of their guns we could start over, reason with them. If I ordered you to go back, would you?"

"Yes," Zip answered, his eyes still squeezed tight.

Guilt tested the door of my mind, shook the windows, trying to get in. Should I insist that we go back? Try to save them? From what? Themselves? If they would stop fighting and grow food, they could live just as long on Mars as on Earth. Could Zip and I be some sort of mediators and convince them to set down their arms? No. It was pointless. Finding a handful of survivors on Mars didn't change the fact that humanity had ended. It was a non-significant digit in the equation. I shook my head and sighed.

"It would have been nice to be around another person again," I said, surprised by my own words, having avoided people so thoroughly for so long. Then I looked at Zip. "No offense, buddy."

Zip opened his eyes and smiled at me. "None taken, Wren. This place," he motioned to the receding bubble of light that was the Mars Colony, "is not your destiny."

We rose, faster, through the frictionless waters above Mars, watching Earth and its attendant celestial bodies shrink away daily. I made playing cards out of some paper we found on board and taught Zip to play poker. He was pretty good at bluffing. We made up songs, and to my own surprise, I told him about Sammy.

I wondered if he already knew — about my great shame, my disgrace, the source of my endless guilt. He gave no sign of having known, listening intently with his head tilted in that way that meant he was reading my emotions. I cried and he waited, his face a portrait of patient compassion.

My dreams changed. The shame and horror of Sammy's death kept coming, as always, but instead of lying inert at the poolside, I found myself climbing a ladder into the heart of the sun. The effort of forcing my aching arms to release their rung in search of another before taking the next step made it hard to focus on my guilt, and the friends and family that despised me for what I had done were so far below that it was hard to see their judging eyes.

Jupiter bulged out from its sphere, as large as a continent, a clockwork monument of complex movement. Colored bands crossed its surface and great balls of light hovered around it like fireflies. It gave off a low mechanical hum of such intensity that I was afraid our little ship, dented by the Martian bullets, would fly apart. The Sphere that supported Jupiter was as formidable as the one that carried the Sun, full of crisscrossing struts and beams, but in constant motion, far more active than any of the other Spheres. I stared at it in awe. It was so clearly *doing* something. I could almost recognize it. It hung on the tip of my tongue like a forgotten word. It was making something. Destiny, I supposed.

"Buckle up," Zip said, "this is going to be tricky."

I attached my restraints and was glad to have them as we dashed and spun between the moving segments of the churning apparatus. I couldn't tell if the sub was a deft acrobat or a leaf in a stream. When we crossed the Sphere's outer edge, a giddy feeling rose in my stomach and my body rose up against the restraints. Suddenly the universe flipped. Jupiter spun from stern to aft and Earth, which had been a constant beneath our feet since the beginning, swung around to rest overhead. I flopped back into my seat, disoriented and dizzy.

"What just happened?" I asked.

"Gravity has reversed. The waters above Jupiter have that effect. We will no longer be floating upward through the celestial waters. To reach the stars, we must dive."

Somehow, the fact that our destination was beneath us, instead of above us, had a profound psychological effect. It made the stars seem more remote, as inaccessible as if we were heading to the bottom of a terribly deep ocean. And yet, our goal was far more distant and exotic than that.

Saturn was said to be the most beautiful of all the celestial bodies, but it was nowhere in sight when the Sphere that carried it emerged from the starry background as a rarified web, like filaments of starlight. We passed through it like birds through a cloud or a sleeper falling into dream. It faded back into the stars behind us as we continued our long fall.

Earth shrank to the size of my fist. The bright silver moon was its constant companion and even the

Sun ventured no further than an arm's length from my old home. The sub groaned and creaked in disturbing ways. Even Zip started to have a worried frown on his face.

Finally, he spoke. "The submarine won't be able to withstand the pressure much longer. We have to abandon it before it crushes us and traps us within.

"What? Abandon it? You can't be serious? I'll drown. I —" I stopped myself. I didn't believe my own protests. Some part of me knew that I hadn't needed to breathe since I woke up in the Tinkers' City. I had no doubt that I would survive outside the sub.

Zip watched my protests die off.

"Ready?" he asked.

I nodded, and he concentrated for a moment, popping both latches. Cold water poured in and flooded the cabin quickly. We drifted from our seats and swam up and out into the darkness, watching as the dead, flooded sub fell away from us toward the depths of the starry ocean floor. It was terrifying, falling into the night sky, just the two of us, amidst such vastness.

We found we could still talk, in distorted voices.

"You can control the glass within you to change your form," Zip said, "just like when you controlled the rungs of the upper spire."

It took some effort, but eventually I learned how to reshape my legs into flippers. After some exploratory swimming, we were soon chasing each other and playing like infant otters that had discovered water for the first time. Eventually we grew tired and drifted down, side by side. The darkness deepened and I began to feel the weight of the waters above me. Zip felt it too — from time to time I caught him holding his head and grimacing. In the still silence, questions bubbled into my mind, creating a pressure of their own.

"Zip? Why did the Tinkers send you to me in the form of a dog?" I asked. "Why not like you are now?"

"I'm not sure. Would you have followed a talking automaton?" Zip answered.

"Hmm." I thought for a moment. "Good point."

My next question had been on the tip of my tongue since Mars, but I had dreaded asking it. I knew the answer and didn't want to hear it. But I had to ask.

"When you used the remote sensing equipment back in the Venetian City, did you look at Earth? You know, for survivors?"

"Yes."

"Did you find any?"

"No. None. Earth has been completely empty of animal life since you left it."

We fell in silence, holding hands, for a long time.

"What do you think will happen when we reach the stars?" I asked.

"I don't know. What do you think?"

I remembered my mother all those years ago. *Touch a star, baby, it'll make everything better.* What would that look like?

"I don't know. But it seems a shame," I said, looking up through the Spheres, "for all of this to be empty forever. For there to be all this beauty, with no one to appreciate it."

"Do you?"

I looked at Zip, illuminated as much by the Stars as the distant Sun. "Do I what?"

"Do you ..." The delicate spinning flywheels behind his jaw had stopped moving. His chest plate was sunken, and he had a faraway look in his eyes.

"Do you ..." he said.

"Zip, what's wrong?"

I held his shoulders and felt the creaking of his chest plate straining inward.

"Oh, no. No. The pressure. It's killing you. We have to go back. We have to go up! C'mon." I grabbed Zip under his arms and kicked furiously against our fall. I felt the water push back against my flippers and the strain of the effort in my legs, but had no way of knowing if I was making any progress.

His eyes swiveled to meet my own. "No. Wren. You must keep going." With a sickening shudder his skull plate crumpled and his eyes went dark.

I kicked against the water for a long time after that, begging Zip to answer. Eventually, there could be no doubt that he was gone, and I stopped.

"We were supposed to be together until the end," I said softly.

We fell together for a long time and I waited for the waters to crush me too, but the pressure had no effect on me. The glass was all through me, he had said. Suddenly I was furious. Why hadn't the Tinkers given the same protection to Zip? They must have known this would happen. Only one answer made sense. They wanted me to be alone. But why? Was I destined to be alone forever? A profound sadness settled over me as I fell toward my mysterious destiny among the Stars, clutching the husk of my friend.

Far overhead, the Earth was no larger than a marble; it was beautiful, serene. The silvery Moon kept close to its beloved Earth, while Mercury and Venus dashed playfully back and forth across the Sun. Earth cycled from crescent, to disc, to crescent, to blackness as the Sun swung around it, over and over. Achingly slow at first, the dance of the celestial Spheres gradually accelerated. I closed my eyes, letting their movements permeate my mind the way the glass permeated my body. From here, the connections between all its parts were obvious. The Cosmos was a living organism and humanity had given it consciousness. It was sleeping now.

A fluttering light caused me to open my eyes. The Sun was circling the Earth so quickly that its light flickered. It moved faster and faster until it became a fixed ring of light around the Earth. Years were passing between heartbeats. I remembered now — the waters above Saturn slowed time. The deeper I fell, the slower time passed for me. I would never reach the stars. Time would slow, and slow, and slow the closer I got. It wasn't possible to touch a star.

What did that mean? Had I failed at whatever the Tinkers wanted of me? Had they known I could never reach their goal? Did it mean that I could never heal?

But I had healed. Somewhere between Earth and here, I had forgiven myself. The wonders I had seen, the feeling of connection I felt, these had sapped the guilt of its strength and exposed it for the cruel madness that it was. Even when I was a child, the healing had never come from actually touching a star, it had been from the act of trying.

I squeezed Zip against me, closed my eyes again and felt the Spheres tugging me, each in its own way. All the parts of the Cosmos, connected, singing our song, together. Then I felt it. On Earth, but connected to me and everything else, as all things are. I felt something there, looking upon the Cosmos with the same awe I felt now. A new creature, not human, not even close, had risen from the ashes of the animal kingdom and was filling the world with self-awareness. It began as a flicker, then grew and grew.

The Cosmos was waking up again.

And the Firmament would be in danger again. It still hadn't healed from what we had done to it, and soon these new creatures would be at its gates. Maybe they'd behave more responsibly. Maybe they'd be able to figure out what happened to us, learn from it, and avoid the same fate. Maybe. Or maybe the same cycle of destruction would go on forever without survivors of one era to warn those of the next.

If only they had someone to guide them. If only the Firmament had a defender. A voice. Someone to protect it until the new civilization was wise enough to take care of it properly. Could I do this? Could I face eternity alone? The alternative was clear; I knew the glass within me would obey if I told it to end my life. But the Tinkers had been right; I did not fear solitude. Loneliness was a familiar enemy, and it would feel good to have a purpose.

I held Zip's lifeless body at arm's length. "Thank you, my friend, for showing me these things. I understand, finally, why the Tinkers sent you." Gently releasing my grasp, I let him fall away from me. I watched as he grew smaller with distance until I could no longer see him against the starry background. Then I turned my gaze upward and started kicking my way back up.

When I arrived, the Venetian City was already humming with life. Everything — all the factories, sensors, monitors, and libraries —responded to my command. I could create whatever I needed and sent automatons out across the Spheres to make repairs. I hadn't been ready for this role the last time I was here, and Earth's new inhabitants had still been many millions of years away. My attempt to touch the stars had healed me and breathed new life into the Earth.

I discovered that Zip had uploaded his memories into the City on our way through, but they stopped then, before our climb. Our time together on the ladder, and beyond, were mine alone to remember. The Zip I lost beside the stars was irreplaceable, and would always be missed. Still, it was good to have the company.

On Earth, the new inhabitants had grown and expanded across the globe, forming a great civilization. They had invented steam power and it wouldn't be long before they were blowing holes in the bottom Sphere.

I reached down from the monitoring portal and patted the newly reconstructed Zip on the head, then I stood, stretched my back and unfurled my shimmering, rainbow-clad wings.

"Whatdya say, Zip? Are you up for a trip downward? I think it's about time we meet our new neighbors."

He did a little excited loop and sat on his haunches.

"I'll take that as a yes."

"The Firmament" originally appeared in *Reading 5X5 x2: Duets* on August 2020.

About the author

Douglas Anstruther was raised among the long cold winters of Minnesota. At age seven he discovered that there were other worlds beyond our own and was astonished, and frankly disappointed, that no one had thought this important enough to mention earlier – a sentiment he still holds today. At some point he married his lovely wife, Dana, went to medical school, had three very nearly perfect children and moved to Wilmington, North Carolina. When not tending to people's kidneys, Douglas likes to read, write and talk about history, linguistics, space, AIs, the singularity, and everything in between. He particularly enjoys writing stories that will rattle around in the readers' head for a while after the last page has been turned.

www.facebook.com/douglasanstruther, @DouglsAnstruthr

The Preserved City

Charles Schoenfeld

Simona's view of the modern city dropped away as the cable car rose toward *Città Alta*. Above the ancient city wall, she could see black-clad families milling about in the pre-dawn glow. Services would begin in twenty minutes, at 5:00 a.m. Those who had risen early were enjoying the beauty of the upper city, its medieval architecture and narrow cobbled streets unaltered since Renaissance times.

Simona's black shawl rubbed against her lips, and she brushed it away. She had been awake longer than any of her neighbors. In Bergamo—or any northern city —the women did not prepare feasts on All Souls' Day, nor leave their homes open for the spirits. But Simona kept up the southern traditions, even if her grandmother would have cringed to see her preparing portions of that feast in the microwave.

The funicular deposited Simona near the Piazza Vecchia. The other women greeted her warmly as she crossed the square. They asked about her work, which made it necessary to lie. "Making progress," she said.

Two years earlier, most of them had come to see *L'Applauso È Napoletano* in its first few weeks at La Scala. They were not habitual opera-goers, but they knew the composer and took neighborly pride in her success.

It was an easy story for northerners to love. While her opera gave an inevitably nostalgic, romanticized view of Campania, her southern home, it was ultimately a paean to everything Bergamo had taught her to love about the north: its scenic beauty, its air of civilized contentment. The southern heroine does not *return* home in the end; she *finds* home.

Every line of the square's architecture drew Simona's eyes upward—the arches and pillars of the library's white façade, the stony bulk of the ancient bell tower. An archway led to the chapel. Simona found a seat near its acoustic center. Stefano, her fiancé, would be attending services with his family in Milan, an hour away. He had invited her, but she had a plan of her own for this morning, and it could only be accomplished here, in the Basilica of Santa Maria Maggiore.

Simona joined her neighbors in lighting candles for the departed and reciting the prayers. Some of the women who had lost relatives within the past year wept while the organ played.

Simona's analytical facility had outgrown its proper place in her mind. She did not hear the organ music as a unified whole; her ear picked the musical phrases apart into individual chords, and the chords into isolated notes. This rendered the composition meaningless; any arbitrary substitution could have been made, and would neither improve nor damage the music.

A-flat? Why not G?

Half note? Why not two quarter notes?

Composer's intuition, she answered herself. *I used to have it too.*

The mass ended. While the other churchgoers dispersed to tend family graves, Simona made her way to the rear of the church, where lay the one dead Bergamasco to whom she felt any connection.

Simona knew of no more touching monument, anywhere, than the relief carved on Donizetti's tomb. It depicted a group of cherubs at the moment when they heard of the composer's death. Several were bending and breaking their lutes; one, angry-faced, held his lute over his head with both hands, ready to smash it upon the ground; another stood poised to crush his lute beneath his upraised foot. In the center of the relief, a kneeling cherub wept, hands covering his face, while the cherub at left gazed heavenward in despairing incomprehension.

Simona traced the relief with her fingertips, then began to speak.

From its long rest, Gaetano Donizetti's consciousness flickered into existence, so that a sound might intrude upon it. A woman's voice said, "… to pay respect to you on this day."

Inside the tomb, Donizetti's soul formed a vague head-shape and nodded it in recognition. The living often stopped by to honor his memory. On All Souls' Day, when the barrier between worlds was thinnest, he could hear them.

"Great master, offer me guidance—"

Guidance? There was a dangerous word. She hadn't fallen to her knees before his tomb, had she? His senses sharpened; he tried to be certain.

"I have succeeded once. And now, no music I write approaches the beauty of what I've already written. But you, you breathed music as others breathe air—"

Excessive flattery. I worked at my music.

"Teach me to remember what I once knew. Help me to release the music in my soul—"

He formed a face, which formed a scowl. *I joined the army rather than teach music. Know me before you ask these things.*

Her voice was growing ever more frantic. "Don't leave me in this state: silent, unheard. I exist for Music —"

No, no, this is all wrong. An ember of outrage began to glow in the dark of Donizetti's tranquility. *Music should give joy to its creator, never enslave her. Else, why create?*

"Inhabit me, if you can." Her voice was choked. "Make me your instrument. If I can no longer create, I can still ... I can ..."

Must you make me care for you? There should be peace in death.

"I'm sorry, I don't know what I'm saying. Forgive me."

Pity overcame Donizetti at last, if only by a narrow margin. He gathered himself and stepped from his tomb, but there was no one kneeling before it.

Footfalls echoed on the flagstones. He caught the barest glimpse of her flushed, tear-streaked cheek as she ran from the chapel. But today, on All Souls' Day, he could be anywhere within *Città Alta*, instantly. Anywhere that he had been before. So, the barest glimpse would be enough.

Simona walked the narrowest of the old streets, turning her face to the walls until she had composed herself enough to be seen without loss of dignity. She descended to *Città Bassa* via the funicular and went home.

Stefano arrived that evening. His gaze lingered on the feast she had left for the spirits. She'd been composing, and had not yet cleaned it up.

Stefano had advised against leaving her home open all day, but now he refrained from comment. She loved him for all the protective things he obviously wanted to say, and loved him even more for having enough respect not to say them.

She cleared away the dishes and prepared a dinner. While they ate, Stefano told her stories about his family, with whom he had spent the day. His younger sister had a new boyfriend, of whom Stefano did not quite approve. Simona found it adorable that his protective tendencies applied to everyone he loved, not only to herself.

Stefano's older sister worked as an assistant manager in a hotel. She always had hilarious, and sometimes infuriating, stories about the guests, which Stefano recounted in as much detail as he could remember.

For Simona, whose thoughts of late had revolved entirely around her music and how little of it she was writing, Stefano's willingness to carry the conversation came as a welcome diversion. She could forget her concerns for a while, as he chattered on.

Then, for an instant, they were not alone at the table. One of the empty chairs was occupied by a ... trick of the light. But it was a man-shaped trick, with a wild curl of shadow atop its head and another that might have been a bow tie beneath its chin. When she turned to glance at it, one of its eye-shimmers disappeared and reappeared. On a more solid form, it might have been a wink. Then the figure vanished.

"Are you all right?" Stefano asked, breaking off in the middle of a story.

"Hmm?"

He smiled. "You went away for a minute there."

He hadn't seen it, then. "Oh, sorry. I was just wondering ... can you stay the night?" She picked up her empty plate and carried it into the kitchen.

He followed with his own plate. "I hadn't planned on it, but I'd love to. You know I have to wake up early for work?"

"I know. It's just ... there's something a little spooky about this holiday, isn't there? The spirits of the departed walking around? Your presence would be comforting."

She didn't want to tell him what she had seen. For one, she wasn't certain she had seen it. And even if she had, Stefano tended to worry when she had a problem he couldn't solve, or wasn't supposed to.

"And your presence would be delightful," he replied. He kissed her, and she kissed back, made it last longer than he had planned, turned his casual gesture into one full of longing and love.

"Yours too," she said. "Especially if you can get up for work without waking me."

"I'll do my best."

During breakfast the next morning, alone in her apartment, Simona put on her recording of *L'Applauso*. She had not listened to her own work in months. She had polished it so lovingly, and they had found the ideal performer for every role. The recording had captured her music the way it was *supposed* to sound. It made anything different—anything new—seem wrong. She worried that her next work would sound like a soulless imitation of her one great success. That was the easiest thing for reviewers to write about *any* composer's second offering. They almost didn't need to attend a performance.

So instead, Simona's new work accumulated in her wastebasket over the course of each day. Soulless imitation might be an improvement.

She sorted through piles of CDs. *Mozart ... Rossini ... trick of the light.*

There he was, depicted on the cover of a CD. The same wild curl of hair she had perceived as a shadow.

Not a bow tie, but a cravat. Donizetti. And he had winked at her.

She rushed from the apartment without finishing breakfast.

All Souls' Day had passed, and the barrier between worlds had begun to thicken. Normally, it would have taken enormous energy for Donizetti to travel the city freely—the sort of energy that comes from unresolved grievances against the living. Donizetti had no unfinished business, but now he had a connection to a mortal.

They had kept his old bed, all these years. It was on display in his museum, a small, second-floor suite of rooms that also housed his sheet music, instruments, clothing, and other personal effects.

He knew that the woman would come. She had asked for him, and he had appeared. It had taken all of his concentration to make himself visible in *Città Bassa*, even just barely visible, even just for a moment. But he had done it, and she would come.

His old doublet hung on a wooden tailor's dummy. He touched it, let his fingers pass through the velvet, let the feel of it come alive in his memory. Then, with a moment's concentration, he shaped the matter of his soul to resemble it. He repeated the trick with his old walking stick, touching the original and creating a spirit replica that he could hold.

So he lay on his old bed, wearing his old finery, one sole planted on the mattress, his knee pointed jauntily upward. He twirled the walking stick in his fingers, and he waited.

The woman arrived flushed and panting. There was something tentative about the way she walked, the way her eyes traced each surface, wondering if it might be inhabited by a spirit, if ghosts really could exist and answer people's prayers.

When she saw Donizetti, she froze for a moment, taking in the sight of him. She swallowed. "It *was* you," she said. "You came to me."

"And you," Donizetti replied, his nasal voice resonating off the walls, "took your time returning the favor!"

He sprang from the bed in one fluid motion, rapped his walking stick twice on the floor. "Come! We have work to do."

In Florence, which had been home to Leonardo and Michelangelo for long portions of their lives, Donizetti might have been dimly remembered, a historical footnote. In the quiet mountain town of Bergamo, he was the most renowned of the city's sons, the single greatest source of civic pride. One could not spend much time in Bergamo without hearing his name. That was one reason Simona had chosen him to hear her prayer.

Still, praying to the great man's tomb had been one thing. Sharing his company, bearing the weight of his full attention, was another, and far more exhilarating.

"Begin by showing me how you compose," Donizetti said.

"What ... what do you mean?"

"I mean, here is pen! Here is paper! Begin!"

Simona wondered how long their privacy would last. "What about ..." She gestured toward the ticket-taker in the hallway, her back to the museum's entrance.

"These rooms are my domain. She will not hear what I do not wish her to hear. Now, begin."

Simona stood over an exhibit case, drew a staff on the blank page, hummed a few notes, and wrote them down. She ran a hand through her long hair, blew out a breath. Then she wrote a few more notes.

Donizetti stood at her shoulder, watching the pen move.

She paced the length of the main room once, twice. She picked up Donizetti's old violin. Conveniently, the museum kept it strung for appearance's sake. She gave it a cursory tuning, carefully played a few notes on it, and wrote them down. Then she snatched up the paper in one hand. She would have crumpled it, but hesitated, not sure whether she had permission.

The first ruined sheet of the day had come even faster than usual, with Donizetti watching.

He sighed theatrically. "I see. You know quite well *how* to compose. I am not so sure you remember *why*. Come, then." He swept out of the museum. The ticket-taker showed no awareness of him as he passed, but nodded to Simona as she followed.

In the Via Gombito, the ever-present Roaring Old Man tottered by, emitting nonsensical syllables and daring anyone to meet his gaze. He was a fixture in the afternoons; Simona encountered him nearly every time she visited *Città Alta*. "Arrrrhh!" he yelled, and, "Aiieeeee!" He tottered on his way. Donizetti leaned close to Simona and spoke in her ear. "A comic buffoon?" he suggested. "A drunken, declaiming baritone? Or a fallen genius—a strident tenor, lamenting his lost glory? Perhaps a spy, concealed in plain sight? The stuff of opera, in any case. *Compose him.*"

At the fortress called La Rocca, atop a broad tower of sand-colored stone, a stiff wind flapped the Italian flag. Donizetti stood in the center of the stone courtyard and shouted over the wind: "A mighty fortress! A symbol of liberty!" He stepped closer to Simona, lowered his voice. "But it was also a prison, once. And the French used it when they conquered us, and the Austrians too. There is music here. Stirring, patriotic music, and dark, oppressive music."

Simona looked at the fortress, trying to make the music come, but it would not come. She avoided meeting Donizetti's gaze, fearing to admit that she could look at La Rocca and hear nothing.

"Come," said Donizetti.

They climbed the bell tower and looked down into the Piazza Vecchia. Donizetti offered no commentary, seeming to wait for something. As Simona turned to face him, the huge bell tolled, just meters above her head. Donizetti flickered translucent and vanished. The sound took away Simona's ability to think, to descend the stairs, to do anything but cringe, hands over her ears, and wait for the bell to finish.

Finally she descended the tower and found Donizetti waiting. "You looked like you could use a shaking," he said. Simona stared at him in blank amazement, then laughed. Her eyes closed and her chest shook and as the tension left her, she realized it was the first time she had smiled in Donizetti's presence.

They walked along the city wall that divided the upper and lower parts of Bergamo. Simona wondered how *Città Bassa* must look to Donizetti, with its automobiles, with people tapping at their smartphones, skateboarders with their blue spiked hair, chemical plants and apartment complexes made of concrete, glass, and steel. Here stood one of Bergamo's most celebrated ancestors, surveying what his grandchildren's grandchildren had made of themselves. How would he judge it all?

She tried to put the question into words, but the thoughts seemed too large, and the words came out awkward, incomplete.

"I've never thought about it," Donizetti said.

They stopped and leaned against the wall, looking out over the valley. "Behind each window, along every street," said Donizetti, gesturing broadly across the expanse of orange-tiled rooftops that stretched all the way to the mountains, "a life runs its course. All of those lives, orbiting one another like planets, twinkling in isolation like the stars ... and finally, scattered like dust." He blew on his upturned palm. "Compose *them*."

"Have you done anything other than compose today?"

Simona jumped, her pen making a streak across her sheet music. She hadn't heard Stefano enter the apartment. "No, not today," she said. "Today was a composing day."

"It looks like it's been a composing *week*." He started making a circuit of her apartment, picking up her discarded clothing from the backs of chairs, the couch, the floor, the dining table where she now sat working. He carried the clothing into her bedroom.

"You don't have to do that," she called after him.

"Which makes it wonderfully generous of me, don't you think?" He returned, gave her a quick smile that was probably supposed to be charming, and picked up a few of her discarded coffee mugs. He swept off to the kitchen.

Simona turned her attention back to her music. She tapped her pen against the table, trying to focus on the rhythm. Clattering dishes broke through her concentration, as Stefano began washing the ones she'd left in the sink. She stood and went into the kitchen.

"Was I expecting you tonight?" she asked.

"No. But your friend Donna called me and asked if you were all right. I told her I'd check on you."

"Donna called you?"

"She tried calling *you*, last night."

"I know. I wasn't answering the phone. I was—"

"Apparently it was her birthday? And you were invited to the—"

"Oh, *damn*. That was last night."

"It was."

"Great. That's fantastic." She stared at the ceiling for a moment. "Okay. I'll have to make it up to Donna, after I'm done with all this."

"Done with all what?"

"Finding my way through this … this darkness in my mind. The music still isn't coming. It's not like writing *L'Applauso*. That's probably good. I'm not trying to write the same opera over again. But if *L'Applauso* had failed, no one would have noticed. And if this fails, *everyone* will notice."

"People seem to notice when you forget their birthday parties, too." He gave a little chuckle, as if trying to make a joke of it.

"I know. I know what I owe my friends. But I know what I owe my audience, too. And I'm afraid, Stefano. It may be that what I owe them"—she tapped at her breastbone—"isn't in me anymore. What then? What am I supposed to do?"

"Well, I think you could start by taking a breath or two," he said. "Go for a walk, get some fresh air, have a nice meal. The audiences aren't demanding anything right now. You're the one putting all this pressure on yourself."

"No, of course the audience isn't demanding anything. And they won't. Audiences are always willing to forget you ever existed."

"I don't think they'll forget about you in the time it takes to … I don't know … go out for some gelato. Or go to a birthday party when you're invited."

"That's your solution to all this? Gelato?"

"Gelato is the solution to many of life's problems."

Simona rolled her eyes.

"I know it helps me when I'm having a hard time at work," he said.

"It's different for you. You leave the lab at the end of the day, and your work stays behind. It's just something you do; it isn't *who you are.*"

"This isn't who you are, either," he replied. "This is a downward spiral. Look at this place. You're not taking care of yourself, you're not eating well ..." He opened one of her cupboards and removed a package of penne. "Let me cook you a nice dinner—"

She took the package from his hand. "Look, Stefano," she said. "You'll be a good father someday, but don't practice on me. I'm not a child."

"That's not what I—"

"And I don't think I'm hungry tonight." She replaced the penne on the shelf and closed the cabinet. "And I ... I don't think I'm in the mood for company. You should go."

"Simona, you *need* to—"

"Please go."

They stood facing each other for a long moment, each staring at a different spot on the kitchen floor, not moving except for the heaving of their chests as they breathed. Finally, Stefano left the kitchen. A moment later, Simona heard her front door open and close.

She returned to her dining table and began again to compose.

Donizetti took to unlocking his museum for Simona after the building had closed for the night. He never had to wait long for her to arrive. He insisted on candlelight, and on working long past midnight.

"Working through your fatigue will force your inhibitions aside," he said.

"Couldn't I just drink a bottle of wine?"

"No. Artists deprive themselves of sleep. Poseurs drink."

Città Alta had been wired for electricity, but he refused to permit its use while composing. *We must give you an authentic experience, after all,* he thought. *You believe that music must be a struggle. Let us take that belief to its extreme, and see what we may find there.*

"There is no music in these electric lights," he told her, his footsteps echoing in the silence of his museum as he slowly paced. "They don't flicker; they don't dance." He noticed a gutter of wax forming. "They don't weep. They only buzz, steady and atonal. We must surround ourselves with music, and weed out that which is not music."

Simona dropped her head back to the page in front of her and filled a few more measures.

Donizetti had learned to sneak glimpses at the music; Simona could not work while he stared. *Her music is beautiful,* he thought, watching her with sympathy. *Almost as good as mine.* He stepped closer to her and peered down his nose at her current score.

Perhaps better.

She had taken a modern office worker as her heroine. Her introductory scene was ambitious, panoramic. It began with an alarm clock, followed the young woman out of bed, through the horns-and-tubas rush of morning traffic, and into an office building. Percussion imitated the clack of computer keys, the clink of tiny espresso cups against saucers and desktops; strings toyed with the repetitive swoosh of a photocopier, the monotone flickering of fluorescent lights; a chorus of voices brought in the chaos of many distinct telephone conversations. Remarkably, the elements all blended, forming a unified impression that somehow gained in beauty the more hectic it became.

Donizetti stood dumbstruck. She had found the rhythm of her own world, the hidden melodies in those very aspects of modern life he had called devoid of music.

The heroine switched on her computer. Simona wrote: "Sintetizzatore"—synthesizer—then crossed it out, then began to write it again. She gave a cry of disgust, hammered her fist on the desk three times, and snatched up the paper. She crumpled it in one hand and threw it in the trash.

"Well, try again," was all Donizetti said. Encouragement might have helped her, but not in the way she needed.

She stayed there through the night and into the morning, composing and destroying, and did not leave Donizetti's rooms until nearly midday, as the museum began to receive its first visitors.

Donizetti followed her, to her surprise. "Not to worry," he said. "A change of scenery may do you good. Find a rock to sit on. Compose out here. There are no instruments here, but you can whistle."

She turned around to face him, staggering with fatigue. "Please, I need a break."

Donizetti nodded solemnly. *Then I shall break you.*

"All right," he said. "Follow me."

He led her to a restaurant and watched her order a margherita pizza. While she waited for her food, Donizetti stood over one of the other patrons, leaned in close and sniffed at her cappuccino. The woman seemed oblivious.

"Mmm," he murmured to Simona. "Such dark beauty in the scent of coffee. One forgets it as the decades pass. It entices you with its aroma, makes you feel strong even while wearing away at your insides. It is the most dangerous of lovers: the Seductress and the Destroyer. Soprano, perhaps? But slow and sultry in her rhythms. Even in coffee, there is music."

Simona was only half listening. Now that she had stopped moving, stopped working, hunger and fatigue threatened to consume her. The thought of coffee was tempting, but she needed solid food more urgently. Her skin felt tight on her bones, and the ambient sounds had taken on a tinny quality—not much bass, lots of treble.

The pizza arrived. Donizetti stood behind Simona's chair; he bent to position his lips behind her ear. "Good," he whispered. "Now a bite of pizza. Don't rush it. Taste the sunlight that shone on those tomatoes, the wood that fired the crust, the vitality of fresh basil. Yes."

Simona bit off a chunk of the pizza.

"Oh," said Donizetti, sounding rapturous. "In pizza one can taste all the bounty of nature, the benevolence of God. It is life's goodness in microcosm.

"Now: don't eat it. *Compose* it."

Simona's head snapped around to stare at him in horror. "Don't eat—?"

"You have tasted it once. Don't dilute the memory of that first taste."

But I'm so hungry.

Donizetti was relentless: "Feed your music first. You can feed your body afterward."

She stared at the slice of pizza in her hands.

Donizetti straightened from his crouch and looked down his nose at her, ready to issue his ultimatum. "Is this where I belong? You are not the only composer in Bergamo."

He turned away, took a step.

Simona leapt from her chair, reaching after him with both arms. "Wait! Don't go!" Her voice echoed off the nearby buildings. He felt her fingertips pass through the velvet of his doublet and continued walking.

Behind him, Donizetti heard a small crowd detaining Simona, asking her if she felt all right. They could not see him; they would think she had been shouting and clawing at empty air. He allowed himself to fade from her view. Let her reassure them as best she could.

Only after she felt that she had hit some sort of a bottom could they attempt the real work of building her back up.

The crowd would have put her in the hospital if they'd had the power; Simona could see it in their faces. But she never asked for help, so eventually, they had to disperse.

Donizetti, when she found him again by the city wall, had softened somewhat. He looked her up and down as she approached, then said, "You may be right. You need to untwist yourself. Perhaps I have been too strict, depriving you of other composers' music all these weeks. Let your man take you to a concert tonight. Verdi is playing at the Teatro Donizetti, and he is ... competent. Enjoy yourself."

Donizetti vanished, his body distorting inward toward his own navel and shrinking to nothing. Simona wasn't sure, but she thought she heard a popping noise.

Space twisted around itself, and Donizetti felt himself spiraling through it, as if down a drain. Something had him by the soul. He hoped Simona could not tell that his disappearance had been unintentional. He hoped immortal souls could not be destroyed.

He hoped this was not what it felt like if they were.

He appeared with his back to his own tomb in Santa Maria Maggiore, contained by a half-circle of candles. He looked at the priest first, and did not recognize him. The man next to the priest, though, was Simona's lover, Stefano. They both held crucifixes.

"I saw you," Stefano said without preamble.

Donizetti made no reply.

"I saw Simona from below, walking along the city wall with another man one night," he said. "I wondered who you could be. Then her head eclipsed the moon— and yours didn't. The moon shone through your head. I knew immediately. What other spirit than you would she have chosen as her companion?"

"I am not a rival to you," said Donizetti. "I have no desire to—"

"She is unraveling. You had one full lifetime in which to compose. She is not your opportunity to live again."

The priest was chanting softly behind Stefano. Donizetti felt himself being pulled toward the inside of the tomb. The pull was soft, but getting stronger.

"She is an independent soul," Stefano continued, trembling with fury, "not a conduit for you to reclaim your—"

"She is dying," Donizetti said.

That stopped Stefano for a moment. Donizetti could see the doubt in his eyes: *Have we drifted so far apart that I would be the last to know?* Then he stood straighter, as if preparing to close a door in Donizetti's face. "No. She would have told me."

"Not her body," said Donizetti. "But you must have seen it by now." He tried to step forward out of the circle of candles, but met an invisible wall.

"Yes, I have. I've seen her obsessed by work as never before. An obsession to which *you* must have incited her. I've seen her neglecting her health, her friends—"

"Spare me," Donizetti spat. "She's told me of your great concern for her social obligations."

"Is that so?" Stefano's voice dropped to an injured whisper. "Because she's told *me* nothing of you."

"I can't imagine why not. You show such understanding of the work that's important to her."

Stefano turned his face away sharply, as if presenting the other cheek for Donizetti to strike. "Don't presume to judge me," he said. He met the composer's gaze again, his eyes glistening. "You may see her only as a musician. I see her as a whole person. I love her. And her friends, they love her."

"Then tell me: how much love do you think she could give to her friends if she had none left for herself?"

Stefano opened his mouth to reply, and closed it again.

"I would never deny the importance of friends and family," said Donizetti. "Nor do I doubt that they would provide shoulders for her to cry on, as she mourned the death of the music within her. But would they—would you—rather have a Simona who weeps on your shoulders, or one who stands proud, full of life, full of joy?"

"I have not seen that Simona since you arrived on the scene, *Signore*."

"You lost her before I arrived. And you can hardly expect me to bring her back in a day." He opened his palms toward Stefano. "Music is not giving her any joy. She hungers only for more of the fame she has tasted once. I've known fame; I've walked this path. Have you?"

Again, Stefano stood silenced. Donizetti felt the pull from his tomb strengthening still; he fought not to stagger visibly backward. He spoke faster.

"Because if you can heal her, then yes, please, send me back to my rest. But if you can't ... then for the rest of your life, you can look back on this as the night that you, and you alone, chose to consign her best hope to the grave."

Stefano's fist tightened on the crucifix, until Donizetti thought the wood might snap in his hand. Then, of a sudden, he lowered it to his side. He stepped closer to the circle of candles, to within a few centimeters of Donizetti's shimmering face. "You had better be right. About what she needs."

He turned to the priest. "Thank you, Padre. And sorry to have troubled you." The priest lowered his own crucifix and slumped with relief. Stefano extinguished one of the candles beneath his shoe.

Donizetti stepped over the dark candle, out of the circle.

"Thank you for trusting me," he told Stefano.

"Who said I trusted you? I'm a desperate man."

Donizetti nodded and said, "It should not be much longer." Then he vanished.

That night, when Simona met Stefano at the concert, he smiled cautiously and gave her a slow nod that was almost a formal bow. He said nothing in greeting, likely for fear of saying the wrong thing. It felt to Simona like the first meeting of ambassadors after the conclusion of a war.

They took their seats. Stefano, to break the tension, read an anecdote about Verdi from the program. "Have you heard this story before?" he asked. "While writing *Il Trovatore*, Verdi received a visit from a noted critic. He played three tunes from his work in progress, and the critic informed him that they were all absolute, irredeemable trash. 'My friend,' Verdi enthused, 'thank you! This is to be a *popular* opera. If you had liked it, no one else would. But your distaste promises me great success!'"

It was a hopelessly awkward attempt at safe conversation, reading from the program instead of sharing their own thoughts. But it was also a relief, so Simona went along with it.

"I've never heard that," she admitted. "But then, *Il Trovatore* is what, his twelfth opera?"

"It says here his eighteenth."

"Well, then. I hope by the time I've written eighteen operas, I'll have the stature to tell the critics how useless they are, too."

"If I know you, I think you'll prefer their approval, even then."

She smiled, a little ruefully. "You do know me."

She held his hand while the music played, adjusting her grip constantly. Tighter to reassure him, then looser because her palm felt too clammy to inflict on him.

She felt Stefano lose himself in the music when it started. He did not compose, and played with only a hobbyist's skill, but he was a knowledgeable, appreciative listener. Beside her, he closed his eyes. His head drifted from side to side with each swell of the music, like a conductor's baton in slow motion.

Images of written music tumbled through Simona's mind as the orchestra played. For brief stretches, she could stop herself compulsively rewriting the music as it entered her ears. But soon, the concert became just another exercise in composition. She could improve upon the music for a few measures at a time, then her rewrites would dissolve into cacophony—while the original continued to fill the theater with its infuriating flawlessness.

"I'm sorry I sent you away so abruptly the other night," she told Stefano at the intermission. "My work has me on edge, but I never meant to make you doubt our relationship."

"No, I'm sorry," he said. "For trying to protect you from yourself. You were right. Your gift for music is part of what I love in you. I have no business telling you how to write it."

You love me for my music, she thought, *but what if my music is gone?* That thought would not reassure him. So she wrapped her arms around him and said nothing.

They returned to their seats. The second half of the concert proved more trying for Simona than the first. She listened with a feverish intensity, gripping her armrest with white-knuckled force. She listened as if lives were at stake.

She wanted to be uplifted by the music, enlightened, transformed. She wanted the sounds of instruments and voices to part like a curtain, to reveal some large and glorious truth. She wanted a dormant part of herself to awaken, to resonate with Verdi's music and answer it in a voice of her own.

The music was lively and lovely, but she wanted it to be more than it was. It blithely refused, and she felt sick. Betrayed—though whether by Verdi or by herself, she could not be sure.

Am I learning to hate music? Is that what's happening to me?

At the end of the night, Simona had no auditory memory of the concert. She recalled only the gleam of brass, the black of formal wear, the dancing baton.

The next morning, a Saturday, Simona called her friend Donna. She apologized for missing her party and made plans to meet her that afternoon for a belated birthday lunch. Then she went out to find Donizetti and tell him she would not be continuing her studies. She would not frame it as an admission of failure. It would be an admission that the joy had gone out of trying.

She could not find him in his museum, though. Nor was he at Santa Maria Maggiore. Could he have anticipated her decision to abandon the composing life?

She looked for him in each of the places they had haunted: the bell tower, La Rocca, the café on the Piazza Vecchia. She did not expect to find him, but she felt a duty to be thorough.

When she saw the billowing flag at La Rocca, she heard music in her mind, very faintly. She caught herself humming along with it, and made herself stop.

She drifted through the city, meandering toward the path that ran along the inside of the city wall. The sun shone in a clear sky, and a warm breeze carried the scent of autumn through the streets.

What will I do in the next phase of my life? There was optimism in the question, she was surprised to discover.

She wondered again about Donizetti. Had she disappointed him, or had he meant for her journey to lead here? She stopped at the point on the city wall where they had talked before, and tried to imagine seeing *Città Bassa* through his eyes, watching his descendants' headlong rush toward the future.

She sensed him at her side before he spoke.

"Two hundred years ago, that was a field of trees," said Donizetti. "They were just beginning to build houses down there. How do I feel about your automobiles, your Internet?" He shrugged. "How would my ancestors have felt about my pocket watch, when the clock on the bell tower was once the only timepiece in the city? Who were they to judge, and who am I? People are still people, and that is all I ever was."

He turned to face her. "If I may presume to speak for the long-dead, I thank you for preserving our old, familiar home in a position of honor." He looked out over the wall again, and so did she. "But thank you also for continuing to build. I am pleased to see that Bergamo still lives and breathes."

Simona smiled. She turned to look at Donizetti, to thank him for the time he had spent with her—even to kiss him, if his cheek had enough solidity to receive the gesture—but he had vanished.

She had never actually said the words to let him know that their study sessions were at an end. Somehow, he had seemed to know it already.

If he had, in some oblique way, replied to that knowledge, it was without the disappointment she might have expected.

She lingered by the wall for a moment, overlooking the modern city that was now her home, beneath the stately city that had once been all of Bergamo. Then she set out walking. It was nearly time for her lunch with Donna.

The birds that nested in the trees beneath the wall were singing. Simona whistled a few notes back to them, first mimicking, then harmonizing. Until recently, she would have felt an anxious impulse to remember those notes for later, in case they might be the seeds of her next great work. Now that impulse was gone. The birdsong existed in that one beautiful moment—and when the moment passed, it simply passed.

She was still whistling to herself when she approached the restaurant. Donna had secured an outdoor table for them and was waiting. She stood up to greet Simona, smiling.

"You sound like a bird."

Simona looked confused for a moment, then realization dawned, and she laughed. She hadn't noticed herself whistling. "I must have been imitating them."

Simona apologized again for missing the party, but Donna waved it off. "Like I said on the phone, I'm glad you were just doing your tortured artist thing, and not sick or injured."

It was the same restaurant where Donizetti had taken her, just prior to her breakdown. Simona ordered a small pizza, knowing that this time, she would be permitted to eat the whole thing, instead of trying to compose it.

She and Donna had known each other since childhood, and could talk to each other about anything. So when Donna asked her how the 'tortured artist thing' was going, Simona decided to tell her the whole story. It wouldn't have felt right talking to Stefano about Donizetti's ghost; it would only have made him worry. But Donna, after a few moments of understandable disbelief, reacted with simple wonder—and most of all, with interest in the relationship Simona had formed with her celebrated mentor.

"So, let's pretend I believe you," Donna said, "that you could really give up composing for more than a month or two."

"You're so accommodating!"

"Purely for the sake of argument. Have you thought about what kind of work you'll do instead?"

Simona pursed her lips. "I might teach children to play," she ventured. "I know the violin, cello, and the piano well enough to teach them."

Donna nodded encouragingly. "That's good!"

"Maybe write the occasional advertising jingle. Score a few episodes of TV, if I can find out who I need to know."

Donna let a wicked gleam come into her eye. "So you're giving up music to work with ... music?"

Simona grinned sheepishly down at the table. "Well, that's hardly *real* composing, you know? It's more ... are you a chef going for that next Michelin star? Or are you just grilling a quick dinner on your terrace?"

The waitress arrived and set a plate in front of each of them.

Donna sipped at her drink. Simona expected her to continue asking questions about her music, and her identity as a musician—questions for which Simona didn't have coherent answers yet. But Donna must have sensed that it was a tender topic, so instead, she launched into a bit of gossip about her birthday party. Two of their mutual friends had arrived separately, but left together.

"Oh, they're all wrong for each other!" Simona exclaimed with delighted horror.

"Completely," Donna agreed. "But I don't think they'll realize it for a while, so I'm happy for them. It will be a beautiful mistake."

Simona glanced upward. She could see a jet rising into the sky, leaving a thin trail of white across the clear blue. It passed behind the dome of the basilica and continued on its way—a modern marvel slicing across the medieval skyline.

"A beautiful mistake," she echoed. "I have to say, that would be a *great* title for a piece of music!"

Donna raised an eyebrow as innocently as she could. "Really?"

"Oh, sure," Simona enthused. "You could have the lovers who seem all wrong for each other … only in the end, of course, they aren't. Total opposites: one sings high and lively, with a lot of suspended chords. The other sings low and slow, and everything resolves neatly."

"So interesting."

"And the 'beautiful mistake' motif wouldn't only appear in their relationship. You could work it into other parts of their lives, into the set design, the architecture. The costumes."

Donna was biting down on her lip, and Simona abruptly realized she was doing it to prevent herself from bursting out laughing.

Simona leaned back in her chair, shaking her head slightly. "I guess *that* habit isn't going to disappear overnight."

Donna grinned broadly. "Clearly not."

"Sorry."

"You're apologizing to me?"

"You have to understand," Simona said, "I'm not latching onto this idea because I think it's magically going to wash away all of my troubles and turn me into a great composer again. I'm just …"

"Being playful," Donna supplied. "Over lunch."

"Exactly."

If Donna realized that it wasn't quite the first time Simona had playfully talked over a musical idea during one of their meals together, then at least neither of them felt compelled to comment on the last time it had happened, nor on how very far that idea had gone.

"Exactly," Donna echoed.

Simona took a bite of her pizza—and as the flavors burst across her tongue, the world seemed to slow, so she could linger in their perfection. She made a soft noise of pleasure. Her features melted into a serene smile, and her eyes closed.

Donna watched her head sway slowly as if she were dancing, while, in her mouth, the flavors sang.

"The Preserved City" originally appeared in *Metaphorosis* on 13 November 2020.

About the author

Charles Schoenfeld wrote "The Preserved City" after a trip to Italy, on which he visited most of the locations depicted in the story. He is a graduate of the Clarion science fiction & fantasy writers' workshop, and a past finalist in the L. Ron Hubbard Writers of the Future Contest. His short fiction has been published in *Ember: A Journal of Luminous Things* and *Metaphorosis,* and his plays have been performed on stages in Connecticut and Massachusetts.

Where the Old Neighbors Go

Thomas Ha

The man standing on the porch that night seemed like an ordinary gentrifier at first glance: young and tall and artfully unshaven. His jeans were tattered, but strangely crisp, and his shirt was loose and tight in all the wrong places. He had the appearance of someone vaguely famous, like his face could have been in a magazine ad or on the side of a bus. And to anyone other than Mary Walker, he would have successfully passed for a human.

Mary widened the opening of her front door, knowing she could no longer avoid him. She clutched the edges of her stained bathrobe and stared up at the man through the tangle of her grey and white hair.

He smiled, and there was something off, as if his features were meant to be stationary, not stretched in that way. "I thought I should finally introduce myself," he said. "I'm the new neighbor."

The man gestured over his shoulder toward the house across the street. It was an ashen block of concrete and glass, with sharp and modern angles, sitting on a pristine lot with a newly paved driveway. Every time Mary looked at it, she felt nauseous.

"I was wondering what you'd be like," she said.

"And?"

"I don't see any horns," Mary replied.

He laughed, and it, like his smile, seemed out of place. "I was wondering if we could talk, get to know one another. Unless this is a bad time?"

Mary pushed her hair from her eyes and looked out at the dark street. No dog-walkers or joggers in sight. "Why don't you come in?" she said, standing aside.

The man was already through the entryway before she had finished her sentence, peering at Mary's walls and looking around the corner into the den. "What a lovely home," he said monotonously.

Mary tightened the frayed belt of her robe and walked behind him, watching as he ran his fingers along one of her sideboards and around the rim of a decorative vase. He paused at the sectional sofa in the center of the living room, then looked to Mary, as if inviting her to sit.

Mary needed no invitation in her own home. She went to an orange armchair in the corner and dropped into it comfortably, then pointed a bony finger at the sofa. The man sat at her direction, a glimmer of annoyance in his eyes.

"So," Mary began. "You're the one who bought Frank Abra's home."

He nodded. "I met him very briefly after the closing. Nice guy."

"Hm." Mary rested a weathered cheek on her hand. "A lot of people on the hill have been selling lately. But Frank? Didn't strike me as the type."

"Truth be told, I don't know much about him," he shrugged. "I think the house was getting to be too much to maintain." The man glanced at other rooms that were visible from where he sat. "You live alone too, don't you?"

Mary ignored the question. "Frank was getting on in years," she said, scratching at a mole next to her eye with her index finger. "Still, I was surprised—not so much as a for-sale sign, let alone a goodbye. First time I

Where the Old Neighbors Go

knew what happened was when you got rid of the house."

She vividly remembered the day Frank's place had been demolished last spring.

It had started with a rumbling that made her get out of bed and look out the front window. Mary had watched as a slow-moving caravan of construction vehicles proceeded down the road, then encircled the small, Craftsman bungalow across the street.

She had emerged from her home in her bathrobe and marched over the low bushes in her front yard, waving a hand at one of the drivers.

"Hey!" she yelled. "What're you doing?"

"What's it look like?"

"Where's Frank?" She shaded her eyes with one hand and looked up.

"Ma'am, I don't know who Frank is, but he isn't here. You better back up!"

The construction vehicles roared to life, and the ground began to vibrate as they inched across the lawn.

One of the bulldozers began by tearing through the planks of the front deck. It was an uncovered porch that Frank had built with his wife, Callie, in the Sixties. He hadn't had the strength to repair it in over a decade, so the wood splintered and folded like toothpicks as the bulldozer's blade rippled through with no resistance.

An excavator then approached the side of the house and raised its boom, reminding Mary of an animal rearing to strike. The bucket came down and clawed open a hole in one of the walls, bricks raining down onto the dirt. Mary could see into the home through the wound, the lilac-patterned wallpaper in one of Frank's bedrooms shredded. Several minutes later, the wall next to it, adjacent to Frank's chimney, came apart like cardboard.

Mary covered her nose and mouth with her hand, watching as the sections of Frank's house came undone. Even after the machines left, she lingered on the street and walked through the lot where Frank's home had been, a pile of dirt and rubble that was peppered with pieces of what used to hold the house together.

Mary returned her attention to the young man now sitting on her sofa, trying her best to push the image of the ruined Abra home from her mind.

"Did Frank mention where he was headed?" she asked.

"You know," the man furrowed his brow, "I don't think he did. But I'm sure I have his agent's number somewhere if you'd like to get in touch."

"That's nice of you to offer." Mary leaned on the other side of the armchair. "But enough about Frank. What about you? What brings you to the hill?"

The young man stretched his arms over the back of the sofa, making it a point to show how comfortable he was. "I just really like the neighborhood," he said. "Quiet and removed. There's a good energy about it. And the people seem nice."

"Do they?"

"Relaxed, I guess."

"Relaxed," Mary repeated. "I suppose that's one way to put it."

Mary would have described her neighbors as oblivious.

Not one of them had seemed concerned about Frank when he disappeared. For days after his house was demolished, Mary had gone door to door to see if anyone had heard where Frank was, or even that he was planning to leave.

None of the neighbors had answers, let alone cared.

Of course, it might have had something to do with who was asking. Several of them slammed their doors in Mary's face at the sight of her. Others simply pretended they weren't home. Mary could feel their eyes trailing her from their windows, and a few of them who had known Mary from better days, before she had become this way,

Where the Old Neighbors Go

had a certain look on their faces that she absolutely could not stand, as if they pitied her.

"Are you...taking care of yourself, Mary?" One of the older neighbors looked down at her bathrobe with concern.

"What's to take care of?" Mary scoffed. "It's not like I'm having company anytime soon, am I?" She pushed the tangled strands of her hair out of her face. "I'm just comfortable as I am, thank you very much. But about Frank—"

"I'm sorry, but I really don't know," they said. "You please take care, though, okay, Mary?" The door shut slowly, and Mary muttered to herself as she moved on. She made doubly sure to meet every gaze as she marched down the street, before they each turned away, one by one.

One of the neighbors she did manage to catch at the door, a middle-aged man who lived a few houses down the block, listened to her just long enough to hear her mention Frank's name before interrupting.

"If I tell you what I know," he said, "will you stop calling parking enforcement and asking them to tow my goddamn car?"

Mary was used to these confrontations, and she knew that if she wasn't firm about the way things ought to be, the others would walk all over her. Still, she preferred the honesty of this over the feigned sympathy she got from the others.

"If it doesn't have a permit on the dash, I have to call," she replied. "Could belong to some prowler."

"It's *my* car! You *know* that!"

"I really don't like to assume, you know? Anyway, listen, about Frank—"

This door, like all the others, shut on her.

Mary grimaced to herself as she remembered, but paid it no mind. In her several decades of living on the hill, her neighbors had never understood how her watchful eye kept danger away from their homes. But she didn't need their approval to keep things in order.

The young man on the sofa cleared his throat, trying to draw her back into the conversation. "If it's not too much trouble, could I maybe get something to drink?"

"Ah." Mary sat up straight and then pulled herself out of the armchair. "Of course. I've already forgotten basic hospitality. What would you like?"

"Water would be fine."

"Coffee," she said to herself. "It's late, but I think I'll need it for a chat like this. Would you like a cup?"

"Well, actually I said—" the man shifted, seemingly unsure if she was hard of hearing. "Sure. Coffee is fine."

Mary shuffled to the other side of the den, leading the young man, who followed close behind her, through a dining room and into a kitchen in the northwest corner of the house. It was brightly lit, with soothing blue walls and shining tile that Mary scrubbed daily. She pointed absentmindedly to a breakfast nook in the corner, and the young man went over and sat in a chair.

Mary let her fingers run across the marble countertop as she moved around the kitchen in a practiced manner. She took two cups from her favorite, but rarely used, china set, gently placing each one next to the sink before producing a pour-over glass coffee maker from another cupboard and eyeing the curved, transparent body under the light just to make sure that there were no unsightly water marks. She brought out a tin filled with ground coffee she'd harvested from the cherries in the backyard, the earthy, gritty smell soothing her while she continued to assemble what she needed.

As she gathered the accoutrements, her mind began to drift, recalling other times when she used to make things in the kitchen for more than just herself, when the thudding of little feet and high-pitched giggling echoed through the halls, joining the sounds of the sink-water rushing and glasses clattering as she stood at the countertop.

But then Mary remembered where she was again, and more importantly, whom she was with, and the pleasantness vanished.

"Hospitality is important, you know," Mary said, more to herself than the man sitting at the nook, as she focused herself again and removed a coffee filter from the bottom of a small box. "Across all cultures, the code between guest and host is paramount. The Greeks had a special word for it..."

"Xenia," the young man replied.

"Xenia," Mary nodded, pouring the ground coffee on top of a filter and setting a kettle to boil. "That's right. So you're familiar. You have to be at your best, because you never know who, or what, could be visiting you."

"I like that." The young man leaned back, watching Mary carefully as she stood at the kettle.

"In the old stories, some of the worst monsters were the ones who broke that code. Innkeepers that preyed on guests. Bandits who took advantage of generous hosts. It takes something particularly nasty to do that in a home. Homes are sacred."

The water came to a boil.

Mary grabbed the kettle and poured the water over the coffee pot, and the hot liquid dripped down into the glass body, filling it gradually. "Milk? Sugar?"

"Black is fine."

"Black it is." She poured the two cups and brought them over.

The man took the steaming cup and raised it to his lips, blowing gently and about to drink, when he noticed that Mary was watching him. Something about the coffee smelled unusual and caused him to stop.

He laughed, but in a way that seemed genuine for the first time that night—an angry cackle mixed with shock.

Mary drank from her cup and looked back at him. "What is it?"

She knew he had detected it.

Mary always mixed small pieces of aspen bark into her coffee, so that its flavor would seep into the drink. Its effect on ordinary people was negligible, but on things like Mary's visitor, it could have irreparable consequences.

"So much for xenia," he said, staring intently at the dark, rippling fluid in the cup in front of him.

"Had to try," Mary shrugged.

In truth, she knew this visit had been coming for some time. She had lived too long, and too cautiously, to ignore the warning signs.

After she couldn't turn up any information on Frank, she had gone, as she often did, to her other sources.

Mary set out early one morning up a dirt path behind her house toward the peak of the hill that overlooked the neighborhood. There was a wooded area, filled with blackened trees that had been caught in a brushfire long ago, yet never managed to die or sprout new growth. She followed the path for a few minutes before turning off from it, keeping track of small knife marks she had left in certain trunks.

Finally, at the heart of the woods, she found the carob tree, grey and knotted. She came within ten feet of it and stopped.

"I need to talk," she said.

The leaves rustled, and there was grunting from some unseen space within the branches. The shaking subsided, and there was a silence before something emerged.

Yellow Eyes peeked his head out, appearing in the form of a large, black crow with greasy feathers.

"Whatever it is, I didn't do it," he said. "Haven't been near any of the folks, just like we agreed." The bird shuffled along the branch and turned its head, the ring of one of its eyes focused on her.

Mary watched Yellow Eyes closely. There were times when he would start a conversation, then pounce on her without warning. The last time he had done that, he had been wearing the body of a copperhead, and she could not feel her hand for over a year after.

"Spoken like an innocent," Mary said. "But no. Someone new is moving to the neighborhood and seems like your type."

"My type?" Yellow Eyes said. "You'll have to be more specific. Charming? Good conversationalist?"

Mary turned around and began to walk away.

"Wait." Yellow Eyes fluttered down from the branch and to the ground in front of the woman. "I'll tell you anything you want, if you just, you know…"

The bird gestured with his head toward the circle of pale, purple petals around the carob tree, sprouting up from under the grass and weeds on the forest floor, ever-blooming and just as vibrant as they had been when Mary planted them years ago.

Mary had learned at a young age that creatures like Yellow Eyes could never be confronted directly. Instead, there were other ways, mostly forgotten but still passed down in some families, or buried in books, which Mary made some effort to collect over the years. With the right tools and enough time, she knew she could hold her own against them.

In the case of Yellow Eyes, it took patience, but Mary had meticulously tracked him to his nest after he'd first chosen the crow body. She waited until he was away to seed the circle of vervain, then waited months more as the circle strengthened beneath him and bloomed.

This particular seal, the traveler's knot, was one of the better ones she had crafted in her time on the hill. The living pattern of vervain connected him, not just to the mortal form of the bird he had chosen, but to the tree he had made his home. If anything happened to either the crow or the carob, Yellow Eyes would feel every bit of it, and if the damage was great enough, there were no new bodies that could save him from death. It was a terrifying prospect for a creature who was supposed to live forever.

"Tell me what you know, and I'll decide if it's worth your release," Mary said.

Yellow Eyes crept closer, cocking his head one way and then the other. He drew his beak wide and exposed a row of round, human-like teeth, grinning. "I might have heard about someone who's headed this way. But this one, if it is who I think it is, is definitely not my 'type'."

"Meaning what?"

"Meaning, you know me," Yellow Eyes said. "I'm old-fashioned. I like tricks and deals, the art of a good bargain. But these new things that are coming up now—they're emptier and hungrier, no patience for the craft. They don't get any enjoyment out of the chase the way some of us do."

"Then what do they want?"

"What does any monstrous little toddler want? They want to take everything you have, just as soon as they can swallow it."

Yellow Eyes drew closer to Mary. He puffed his chest and spread his clawed feet on the ground, exposing another set of long, dark fingers between his thin crow toes that curled into the dirt.

His tongue flopped out of his mouth as he salivated, growing overexcited.

Mary could see that Yellow Eyes was beginning to forget himself. She moved slowly to the trunk of the carob tree and reached a hand to the lowest branch, thin enough that she could bend it, but substantial enough that it would work for her.

She snapped it.

Yellow Eyes shrieked as the traveler's knot connected him to the sensation of the branch breaking. He dropped to the ground and twisted in pain as if one of his bones had cracked.

"Settle down," Mary said sharply.

Yellow Eyes shrank and gave the closest thing a bird could to a grimace as he breathed through the pain. "Listen," he heaved, "A couple of little Mary Walker tricks aren't going to cut it with this one. He'll break you in half before you can get anything past him."

"Hm," Mary replied, wondering what she would do if that were true. She knew she would have to think this through carefully in advance.

"So?" Yellow Eyes turned his head, wincing. "You asked; I answered. That clears our ledger, I think."

"Does it?" Mary stared down at the creature. "All I learned was that this stranger is tougher than you are, which," she waved at the vervain flowers, "doesn't tell me much at all."

"Oh, come on." Yellow Eyes flapped his wings. "I played nice, and you can't keep me under the power of this seal forever."

"If I survive, I'll give it some thought." Mary headed back toward the dirt path.

"Mary. Are you serious?"

She waved and kept walking.

"This is why no one likes you," Yellow Eyes screeched. "Mary!"

His cawing carried over the hill, and she heard him for most of the walk back through the woods.

But it turned out, in the end, that Yellow Eyes had been right about Mary's visitor.

The young man didn't seem interested in engaging with, outwitting, or deceiving her. He looked down at the cup of coffee in front of him, dosed with aspen, and his resting expression shifted, almost imperceptibly.

His eyes moved very deliberately from the cup in his hands, up to meet Mary's face.

"I prefer it this way," he said. "Really."

Mary began to retort as she stood up from the nook, but the man interrupted her.

"*Sit*," he said quietly.

The old woman felt her body fold into the seat, like a hand had gripped the back of her neck and pushed her firmly into place, forcing her to stare at the man across from her.

"A little bird told me you were going to be trouble," he said.

Mary's brow creased at the mention of Yellow Eyes, but she did her best to keep her expression neutral. It seemed Mary's visitor had more information about her than she anticipated and, like her, had prepared himself in advance of this night.

The young man pushed his cup across the table. "You know, the thing I enjoy most about a fresh brew is the aroma, flavor...and heat. *Pick it up.*"

Mary's hand moved of its own accord, taking his cup and bringing it closer.

"*Pour it on your hand. Slowly.*"

It had been a long time since Mary had met someone with a silver tongue as strong as his. There were ways to fight this kind of persuasion, with enough preparation and the right tonics, but she knew that it was futile now to try.

She tipped the cup and watched as the steaming liquid spilled onto the back of her other hand, which was firmly pressed on the surface of the table. Little splatters of coffee bounced off of her skin as her hand grew patchy, red and white blisters beginning to form. Mary did her best not to react, but her breathing grew faster and shallower as her eyes watered. She bit deep into her bottom lip as she felt the pain searing up through her arm.

Rivers of coffee joined around her hand and cascaded off the edge of the table, splashing to the tile below.

"Does it hurt?" the young man asked. "It's hard to tell with you."

Even though she could not stop it, Mary wasn't powerless. There were methods she had learned, still taught by older members of certain monasteries who were wary of creatures like this, that were used to slow the connection from the nerves to the mind, even if only for a few seconds.

Mary breathed steadily and concentrated on the sharp, vibrant smell of the coffee, recalling the way it often drifted up the stairs and along the corridors of the house, up to the bedroom on the second floor, and how, when it did, she could pick up its bitter fragrance, even when she was wrapped in layers of her thick, down blankets early in the morning. She was transported to those chilly hours after sunrise when someone else was brewing a pot, and she could hear the whistling of the kettle as she kept her eyes closed, still fading in and out of consciousness. She recalled her daughter's footsteps, her tiny hands pressing Mary's cheeks and poking her nose while Mary pretended to sleep for a little bit longer.

Mama?

Mary trembled until the last drop of coffee had run out, but she did not make a sound.

When she opened her eyes, the young man seemed to be watching her intently, masking just a hint of frustration. His gaze turned to the second cup of coffee, still steaming, but before he could speak, Mary knocked the cup with the back of her red, blistered hand. It flew off the table and shattered on the kitchen floor with a burst that soaked the floor.

The man crossed his arms. "Now why would you do that? I could just make you refill your cup from the pot, you know."

Mary gripped her burned hand and stared silently.

The man moved over in his chair to a spot at the table that wasn't dripping with coffee. He rested his elbows on its surface and put his chin on his clasped hands. "Go on," he said softly. "Cool that hand. And while you're at it, clean this up."

Mary went to the sink and ran her hand under the cold water. She grabbed a wet cloth from a rack and wrapped her fingers, then took another rag to wipe up the coffee.

"I really meant it earlier, you know," the young man said as he watched her clean the floor. "This is a lovely home. Nicer than I would have expected from the way you keep yourself."

"Thanks," Mary replied dryly, throwing the fragments of the cup in the trash and wringing the rag out in the sink.

"It's obvious you have a real reverence for all these *things*," he waved at the furniture and the decorations surrounding him. "You've practically built a museum here, of fonder times perhaps?" The man gave a knowing half-smile and picked up the other cup on the table, holding it to the light and peering at the sides and the bottom. "But no matter how much meaning and memory you imbue these things with, they'll eventually fall apart. Just like you."

He let the cup drop from his hand and crash to the tile floor below, its pieces scattering in every direction.

"Prick," Mary muttered, getting back on the floor.

"What was that?"

She huffed as she stood, then wiped the table in the breakfast nook before throwing the last few shards away. "You heard it."

"You know." He sat forward. "I could burn this place to the ground, with you still in it. And I wouldn't even have to blink."

"Not likely," Mary replied.

"What?"

"Not likely," she repeated. "If that were true, you'd have done it. You wouldn't waste your time with this coffee and small talk," Mary said. "It's clear you want something from me, or I'd be dead."

His eyes darkened. "Maybe this is it. Maybe I want you to suffer."

"Not likely."

"Stop saying that."

"You would have picked a budding young woman to torture or a family to harass. But an old lady like me has no value, and no value, no entertainment."

The young man tapped the table with his fingers.

"We both want this over with, don't we?" she asked. "What's the point in dragging it out now?"

The man appeared loath to admit it, but Mary could tell that he was growing impatient. After a minute of silence, he reached into his jeans pocket and pulled out a piece of paper, unfolded it and put it down for Mary to see.

She picked it up and read it over as she sat down across from him again. "A quitclaim?" she muttered. Mary studied the language of the document a second time. It was a run-of-the-mill human deed for her property, as far as she could tell. Mary had seen a lot of gambits by his kind, but never anything so pedestrian.

"What could someone like you want with my land?" she asked.

"Doesn't matter." The young man's face went purposefully blank. "But the fact that this also gets you out of this neighborhood now strikes me as a bonus."

Mary ignored the insult and read the document again, trying to guess at what the man was leaving unsaid. She assumed that if he could have forced her to sign, he would have already, but something prevented it. He could try to charm, frighten, or bully her, but, in the end, he wanted this transfer to be voluntary for some reason.

"What about the formalities?" Mary asked. "Price, notarization, things like that?"

"The price is whatever you tell me it is. The rest I can make happen tonight, once you sign. It's just paper, after all."

"And is this the deal you made with Frank Abra?" she asked.

The young man stared back without answering.

Of course, Mary already knew what had happened to Frank without the man saying anything. Weeks after the Abra house was demolished, Mary had visited the lot across the street after sundown, when the construction workers were gone.

She had seen that most of the rubble had been dumped, and a giant pit was ready to be filled with concrete for the house's foundation. Mary brought an old metal detector she had gotten at a garage sale years earlier, barely used except for clearing out rusty nails and other debris in her garden. She paced across the Abra lot, waving the detector around, mostly finding coins and scrap, until she eventually came across a piece of jewelry a few feet from where the new house was to be built.

She reached down and pulled a window locket from the soil.

Mary wiped it with the sleeve of her bathrobe and inspected it. She remembered seeing Callie Abra wear the locket every day as she stood out on the lawn and watered their garden, and, after she passed away, Mary saw Frank put it around his neck too, never once putting it aside or taking it off, always grasping it like it was the most important thing on earth. The fact that it was here, and he wasn't, told her everything she needed to know.

Mary slid it into the pocket of her bathrobe and looked around at the lot one more time.

The truth was that she and the Abras had never really been that close. On the best days, she was polite with them, and on the worst, the whole street could hear their screaming matches.

And yet, Mary realized, as she knelt in the dirt, that the neighborhood felt quieter and lonelier without them.

Her fingers crept to the ground, and she touched the soil, feeling its dampness.

Mary remembered the soil as she stared at the young man in her kitchen, thinking of what best to say.

"What will happen to the neighborhood?" she asked him.

"What?"

"The hill. What will you do to them?"

The man shifted in his seat and squinted at her, as if puzzled by her question. "You know, when I first moved here and asked around, it was funny. I didn't even have to pry. Yours was the name that almost inevitably came up when people talked about this street."

"Guess I'm popular," Mary replied flatly.

"Lady Bathrobe," he said. "The Hag on the Hill. Old Tangle-Hair. The Parking Permit Crusader. The Groaning Crone."

"A couple of those are clever, but the rest are objectively bad."

" 'Nobody cares about her,' 'Lives alone for a reason,' they told me." The young man watched Mary sink visibly in her chair. " 'Why doesn't she do everyone a favor and just die?' "

Mary squeezed her burned hand.

"They don't even want to look at you. Just the sight of your filthy robe and ratty hair puts them on edge. Most of them wish you would just disappear and never come back." He shook his head. "I know I'm not telling you anything you don't already know."

"So what?" she said softly.

"So, why do you care what happens to this place after you leave?" The man pushed the deed closer to Mary. "You don't need this hill, and if I've learned anything, it's that the hill *certainly* doesn't need you."

Mary lowered her chin and reached into the pocket of her bathrobe. She felt for the Abras' locket, which she kept there now out of habit, and she touched its smooth, metal edges. For the first time, she didn't have a pithy response for the young man, and he seemed pleased.

"How about, instead of pouring your energy into this house and this hill, maybe you take care of yourself, for once, and enjoy those golden years?" He pinched the sleeve of her tattered bathrobe and smirked. "Because whatever it is you're trying to preserve, it's gone, lady. You've got to see that."

The young man seemed like he was finished speaking and sat back down. Nothing about what the man said changed what Mary was going to do next; in truth, she had made that decision some time ago. But still, when it was quiet again, Mary realized she felt a chill, one that usually visited her when she couldn't fall asleep, and it touched her more deeply than anything else that had happened that night.

After a few seconds, Mary stood and began to walk from the kitchen. The young man followed her, through the study and dining room, and back to the den. Mary approached one of the windows at the front of the house and moved back a heavy curtain, so that she could see across the street clearly.

"There." She pointed at his home, the block of concrete and glass, its modern architecture and chic exterior, like a blight on the hill.

"What about it?"

"You want me to sign? Then I want something first. Whether I leave or not, I can't stand the idea of that shitbox sitting there instead of Frank's place. Makes me sick." Mary gestured over her shoulder. "So let's see if you were telling the truth. Burn it to the ground without blinking, or whatever it was you said."

The young man raised an eyebrow and looked out the window. He was strangely hesitant, and Mary could see that it was her turn to press him.

"That's what I thought," she laughed.

"What?"

"Acting smug and lecturing me about the meaning of 'things'. But I can see it, you're just as attached as I am. Bet you picked the design of that place because you saw it in some magazine. Maybe that's how you picked your face too. All you ugly little fiends just want to be pretty deep down, after all."

"Don't be ridiculous," he scoffed, seeming to grow more self-conscious by the second, as if even the vaguest accusation that he shared anything in common with Mary were perverse.

"Go on," Mary grinned. "It doesn't matter to you, does it? You'll still have the land. Just burn that monstrosity on top of it, and I'll believe you're serious about your offer. I'll sign the deed, just like you want, and we can call it a night and stop wasting everyone's time. What do you say?"

Now it was his turn to go quiet.

"Unless..." Mary looked out the window. "Your whole scheme was to build a suburb of shitboxes, because you love playing house so much? Maybe that's the problem?"

The man eyed Mary, trying to understand why she was being so insistent, but his expression began to change, his pride and his eagerness to finish things winning out. Before he had uttered a word, she knew that she had him.

The young man looked back out the window and nodded his head.

The flames across the street erupted suddenly, from no single source.

In seconds, the entire concrete and glass house was surrounded by a growing fire. The stone did not burn, but the supports and framing inside began to split and crack as the heat spread.

Mary looked over at her visitor, holding her breath.

He began blinking rapidly, and he touched his throat.

Part of the living room of the concrete house tumbled as a support beam crashed to the ground. Some of the glass at the front of the house began to ooze into liquid, pouring onto the lawn, while furniture inside the structure shrank and collapsed.

"Does it hurt?" she asked. "It's hard to tell with you."

The man opened his mouth to respond, but his voice was only a rasp.

The young man staggered out of the den and toward the front door.

Mary watched from the window as he stumbled across the street toward the flaming house, his silhouette twisting and stretching as the fire raged in front of him.

She imagined that as he stepped across the lawn, he finally noticed, hidden among the blades of grass, the pale, purple vervain flowers, just beginning to bloom— the ones she had planted late at night, well before the foundation in that place had been poured, when she had wandered onto the Abra lot, so small and scattered that they probably never caught his eye before.

She still remembered the sensation of the soil, the dampness of it, as she placed the seeds around the property in the right formation, the beginnings of the traveler's knot that would eventually, quietly bind him to that body and to that home.

The young man now turned to look at Mary in the window. There was no time to return to her house and try to compel her to release the bond of the traveler's knot, and even if he could stop the flames, the house was too far gone, the inside of the structure crumbling, much as the insides of his body likely were. The young man knew, just as Mary did, that it was too late now to avoid what was coming.

His face began to collapse, like desiccated dirt, and his true appearance emerged from what remained of his head. Mary always had trouble seeing the real faces of his kind, but he, like all of them, looked like a shifting pool of ink to her, blurred and shapeless.

After a moment of stillness, he looked away and continued forward into the house, moving through a gap where one of the large floor-to-ceiling windows had melted away. Mary could only guess, but as he went further through the flames, she thought he was trying to hide himself, not wanting to give anyone the satisfaction of seeing what was happening to him in his final moments.

He stood with his back toward Mary as everything came apart around him, his tall shape disappearing in the crackling and roaring that filled the concrete block as the fire stretched to the glowing, night sky.

Mary went to her porch and sat on the top step, covering her mouth and nose with the wet rag on her hand. Other neighbors were at their windows, or on their front steps as sirens drew closer to the bottom of the hill.

As she watched the sky darken, a vast cloud of smoke growing above the neighborhood, a crow with greasy feathers landed on the eaves above her.

"I don't understand," Yellow Eyes said. "You had him in a knot. You could have struck a deal, made him grovel, work for you, even. Why?"

Mary did not turn away from the flames. "Maybe he did something to piss me off."

Yellow Eyes watched the fire, as entranced as everyone else.

"Next time you try to play both sides, you'll remember this, though, won't you?" She looked at him coldly.

The crow turned a solid yellow ring of its eye at the old woman, flexed his wings, then took off toward the top of the hill without another word.

By the time the ambulances and fire trucks arrived, a couple of the house's walls were leaning and another had fallen. Everything inside had already been consumed.

There was, in Mary's mind, nothing more to save.

In the days after that fire, Mary returned to her daily routine. Standing each morning on her lawn with a cup of coffee, she scanned the dashboards of the parked cars on the street for any without a permit, then she walked down the block to see if any recycling or trash bins were put out early or left too late, in violation of the county code.

When she wasn't watching for unusual cars or strangers entering the neighborhood, she found herself staring at the charred walls of what used to be the concrete house across the street, imagining the old Craftsman in its place while she gripped the Abras' locket in her hand.

Frank would have come slowly down the steps on each of those mornings to retrieve his mail, gripping one of the handrails—sometimes nodding at Mary and sometimes not. But instead, there was nothing but an ugly view of grey rock and blackened wood. Even now, no one was asking where Frank went, Mary realized, and it was unlikely that any of them ever would.

No one ever asks where the old neighbors go, she thought.

Despite herself, Mary continued to dwell on what the young man said to her the night of the fire. As she dusted her sideboards and vases, she often lost interest, like everything had become too tiresome to finish. When she felt that way, Mary wandered upstairs, to one of the quiet rooms that usually sat untouched, the bed inside still perfectly made and flowery wallpaper around it covered with soft light that flowed through sheer curtains.

She knelt in front of a trunk, unlatching and lifting it open, and peered down at a cluttered pile of old dolls and wooden toys, all of them associated with some holiday or birthday that came back to her as she brought her fingers lightly over them.

In those instances, Mary sometimes considered, for a brief moment, finally throwing them out. Her daughter was never going to use them, after all—she would never brew a pot of coffee for Mary downstairs, or chatter away with her in the kitchen while sitting at the breakfast nook, or touch Mary's cheek to wake her up.

Things would never be like they were again, she knew.

But still, she couldn't bring her hands to move, to take anything from the trunk, and she sat paralyzed for longer than she expected. She kept imagining the young man, standing in front of the roaring flames, and thought, for some reason, that she too might begin to crumble and collapse inward, to fall apart bit by bit, if she were to alter anything in the house, no matter how small.

So, instead, Mary put everything back, got on her feet, and then closed the door to the room behind her— each time, more intent than before to leave things in their place, exactly as they were.

"Where the Old Neighbors Go" originally appeared in Metaphorosis on 11 September 2020.

About the author

Thomas Ha is a former attorney turned stay-at-home father who enjoys writing speculative fiction during the rare moments when both of his children happen to be asleep at the same time.

@ThomasHaWrites

Lighter than Air

Liam Hogan

The aliens never land until they're dead, and I'm about to find out why.

A-Gees, we call them. Some people think that stands for "Anti-Gravity", but they're wrong. It's "Aero-Gels". Their floating cloud-cities are built from a substance literally as light as air. They get their lift from school-bus sized cells of hydrogen gas. Cells that detach and drift between their cities, or that cluster together to form new clouds entirely.

They're here to save our planet.

The A-Gees are galactic *experts* at processing huge volumes of atmospheric gases. They filter *everything* they need from the air, to live, to build, to grow. Easy enough for them to get rid of what we *don't* need, in exchange for a new planet to co-habit.

But dropping their dried-out corpses like discarded litter was *not* part of the bargain.

"Dead weight," is all they post when our bureaucrats try to remonstrate with them on Twitter. The A-Gees have a social media presence, have done from the start. Despite their growing numbers, almost six hundred cloud-cities by now, they're mostly silent. They listen but rarely respond, and then only in fragments no more substantial than their floating cities.

I suppose we don't entirely *mind* if they have to drop their dead, it's a small price to pay to fix our self-induced eco-disaster. But can't they do it somewhere *less* inconvenient? A tumble of dried skin and hollowed bones is not a *good* thing to have land on a kindergarten playground, even if it's more likely to terrify than to hurt. The same for A-Gee corpses wedged on the glass roofs of shopping malls until the winds get around to dispersing the feather-light fragments. Not a fun thing to see, *even* at Halloween...

Can't the bodies be dumped over the oceans, we politely ask, or over forests, or at a pinch, over farmland?

But the A-Gees don't *appear* to understand. Any more than they understand international borders, flight corridors, or increasingly desperate attempts to compare or discuss or exchange technology. The A-Gees go where the winds take them.

Fortunately, a radar-reflecting cloud the size of a small town is not difficult to track; their drift not too difficult to predict. There haven't been any aircraft related accidents *yet*.

And our government's renewed attempts to talk to the A-Gees have an unexpected result. I'm invited to go up and meet them. *Me*, Jess Silver, teenager and vlogger!

Turns out the A-Gees are silent fans of "Ag-Geek" or "Silvergeek" as my stream is commonly known. They enjoy my nightly video pieces, my frothy mix of high school mini-dramas and musings on science and world —mainly climate-related—affairs.

All news to me as I'm dragged out of a drowsy Tuesday afternoon biology class, panicking about what I might have done, or worse; what terrible calamity has befallen my family, until the principal kindly puts me out of my misery. And, other than a pit-stop to get stunned parental permission and gather my video kit, I've been travelling ever since.

We're going up to meet the A-Gees at the oldest and largest of the cloud-cities, currently floating somewhere over the Mediterranean. A small committee of carefully picked diplomats, a handful of chew-their-own-legs-off-for-the-opportunity scientists. And, somehow, *I* get to tag along. Me!

None of the big-wigs are happy I'm there—they make *that* abundantly clear, but my attendance is non-negotiable for the A-Gees. If the big-wigs want a pow-wow, I'm along for the ride.

The final and scariest stage of my half-way round the world journey is by helicopter. A massive ex-military thing far too heavy to set down on a floating cloud, so we get to abseil to a jutting out platform where the A-Gees await. I'm delighted my braids and my snug jumpsuit fare better than the uptight politician's toupees and power suits and flappy ties. Score one to the vlogger.

But I *do* worry that I'll be stuck in boring meetings as policy advisors thrash out some mutually beneficial agreement, all while hoping to avoid an interstellar incident. The prospect almost makes double Math look attractive.

Thankfully (for the politicians as well as for me!) I'm not there for the negotiations. To the envy of the scientists, I'm getting a guided tour of this floating city. The first and *only* human to see behind the scenes. Silvergeek is going where no-one—well, no *human*—has gone before.

You've seen pictures of the A-Gee. Usually described as a half-starved pterosaur without the wings, as drawn by a not particularly talented third grader. Pictures don't do them justice. They might look like something out of a sci-fi show with a strong horror vibe, but my guide moves with an economy of effort that is shockingly graceful. I feel clumsy and slow and *heavy* in comparison. And I am; they've had to give me something like snowshoes to spread my load. Which isn't that great, for a human, but here I weigh the same as a house! That's why the human visitors are always so carefully marshalled. The aero-gel walls are incredibly strong but they're simply not designed for humans. A diplomat going for a wander off-piste could end up doing serious damage, or worse; plummet through the fragile material to the earth far below.

In a half-dozen previous meetings between humans and A-Gees, the humans were carefully herded between rooms created for the purpose, with strengthened floors and human-shaped furniture. By all accounts the negotiations are tiresomely slow. Every so often an A-Gee will get up "to consult with the ancestors", returning an hour later with either agreement or some new and unfathomable condition. Plenty of time for my tour.

"My name," the guide says with something like a curtsey, "is Li-La."

"I'm Jess," I say. I think about sticking out my hand, but decide not to. *Follow their lead* was the scientists' most useful advice.

There's a small motion of her—or his—bird like head. "I am aware. I watch, on screen. Jess; one instruction please. *Observe. Listen.* Ask no questions."

And that, I think to myself, is why I'm getting the grand tour and not one of the nosy exobiologists. Because the A-Gees are *people*, not exhibits in a zoo. We have no idea what taboos they have, what harm a careless query might cause. But they've twigged—no doubt through our social media—that there's a great deal of curiosity about them. Questions a vlogger may not answer, but I'll do my best.

So I do what they've asked of me, honoured and excited by the privilege. I *observe*. My shoulder cam a little ahead of me, one lens trained on my face, the other on what I'm seeing.

Instead of entering the meeting hall with the rest of the delegation, we head down steps no wider than my snowshoes. Cloudshoes? I take my time, unsure what would happen if I tumble.

The bottom, widest layer of the city is where the air gets filtered, Li-La explains. What they don't use is expelled from the centre of the cloud and helps maintain altitude. It can even be directed, either to navigate or to counter light winds if they want to hover in place.

Li-La tells me what they mainly strip from the air is water. I'm handed a small cup to taste. It is cold and pure. Refreshing.

Like humans, A-Gees are mostly water and, like humans, it also forms the the basis for most of their industry. But they're busy devouring everything *else* the air contains as well, including our unwanted pollutants.

Their aero-gels are carbon based. The A-Gees prefer to generate them from methane rather than carbon dioxide, which the earth scientists are more than happy about. Methane is a hundred times worse a greenhouse gas than CO_2, even if CO_2 sticks around for longer. A-Gees *love* methane and when weather conditions allow they hover as close to its sources (swamps, rubbish dumps, warming tundra) as they can.

Eventually they'll need to start harvesting the excess CO_2. The A-Gee-Human contract, their rights to colonise our skies, come in return for helping us achieve a reduction to three hundred parts per million, a level not seen for well over a century. We humans also have to go carbon neutral, of course, which we're still some way from managing. And that's why the scientists want to know how the A-Gees do what they do.

I doubt they'll get many clues from the video I'm streaming. There are no machines, no giant vats. I get the impression all their chemistry happens at some nano-level.

We return to where we started. Stood outside the opaque wall of the meeting room, hoping this is not the end of the tour, Li-La hands me a pair of goggles. When I slip them on I can *see* through the wall, see, in Technicolor hues, the humans and A-Gees gathered around the table beyond. There doesn't appear to be a lot of activity so I suspect they're yet again waiting on some ancestor's advice.

This respect is hard to reconcile with the casual treatment of the bodies of their dead. Though perhaps A-Gee souls are lighter than air. It wouldn't surprise me.

With a start I realise this infrared shifted view must be what A-Gees see all the time, or why else give me the goggles? They must have virtually no concept of privacy. As I turn my head away from the deliberations I see movement all along this level; hundreds of A-Gees going about their daily business.

I glance down but that turns out to be a bad mistake. The world spins lazily beneath me. Gingerly I hand the goggles back. Li-La accepts them without a word.

We head up, the steps broader and shallower, the light brighter. The sunlit top of the cloud is where the hydrogen cells are stored. That's what all the water is for, Li-La explains. Photolysis. And despite the altitude, I haven't had any trouble breathing. The air must be rich with surplus oxygen.

We come to a spot at the very edge of the cloud. It's not for those with a fear of heights and I'm glad I'm no longer wearing the goggles. The bay I'm standing in is open to the elements and gently sloping and I can't help hugging the wall, for fear of slipping. Li-La stands by my side, which makes me feel less like a scaredy-cat.

It's a fabulous view even so. Far below the Mediterranean sea sparkles. I can glimpse islands, ships, even another floating city nearby, a solitary cloud in an otherwise cloudless sky.

Odd to think it's a mere seven years since the deal was brokered by galactic powerhouse the Yrill, seven years since the first A-Gee city—*this* city—was delivered by one of their massive interstellars. How quickly the cloud-cities have spawned and spread!

Some conspiracy theorists claim we're being invaded by stealth, but it's hard to consider the A-Gees any sort of a threat. They don't seem to be interested in anything happening below, their technology lacks anything that resembles either weapons or defence. And without them emissions would still be rising instead of finally showing signs of levelling off. By the time the A-Gees reach peak population, as agreed in the treaty at twelve thousand cloud-cities, CO_2 levels will be in reverse, the climate disaster largely averted.

A single cell approaches as I'm staring out over rocky islands—somewhere near Greece? And then I realise the blimp is heading straight for us. It's not just a viewing gallery; it's a docking bay. Or perhaps, more simply, it's the *absence* of a hydrogen cell.

It's not clear why there is so much exchange between the floating cities, but such cells are always coming and going, whenever two cities are within a dozen miles of each other. Perhaps they carry passengers?

I watch and so does my camera, as the cell fits itself to the waiting hole. There's a noise like mud sucking, a squelch of semi-transparent liquid that fills with fine snaking tendrils, knitting the edges together. Swiftly the cell is indistinguishable from all the others around us, our view gone as we stand in the corridor between.

"An ancestor wants to talk," Li-La says, part of a wall shrinking away. I wait to see who or what emerges, but instead Li-La urges me forward.

Carefully I step through the oval doorway. There's no-one there, as the portal shrinks and vanishes. I wait. And *wait*. I think about switching the camera off to save power and to avoid boring my viewers. Finally, I sit.

"Jess Silver," a soft voice says. "Thank you for coming. I very much enjoy your channel."

I jerk back to standing and the voice fades.

It's coming from the floor.

And, I realise, the walls, and the ceiling.

Cautiously, I lie down, resting my head on the soft pillow surface. And then I listen.

I never pay attention to the comments my video posts get. A schoolgirl fascinated by science is like a red rag to a troll and there are no shortage of haters. But when you're plastered across the newspapers or picked up on the evening news, it's harder to ignore.

There are different reports, different interpretations, of the recording I made. The voice I heard in my head—transmitted by vibrations of the floor?—does not show up on my shoulder cam. So it looks like I'm having a one-sided conversation with myself. Not much to watch either; a featureless ceiling and me, blissed out, eyes alternatively wide or shut, lots of soft "wow!"s and expressions of wordless wonder.

Some commentators say I must have been having a hallucinogenic trip, either because I was a drug addled teenager, (as if!) or because the aliens spiked me, presumably with that cup of crystal clear water. Others take it as evidence the whole A-Gee thing is an elaborate hoax (not elaborate enough to add a distorted sound track for the words of the aliens, though?)

But, as I watch the video back, I can still mostly fill the silent gaps with what I was told up there in the artificial cloud. Not the exact words, but what I *learnt*; what I pieced together.

I'm no scientist. I'll freely admit most of this is conjecture, pure and simple. But I think, I hope, I understand.

I've always loved butterflies.

The hydrogen cells, *they're* A-Gees too.

The whole city, from top to bottom, every wall, every corridor, *everything*, is A-Gees. Like drones in a beehive, each A-Gee has its job, its part of the whole, its role in the cloud.

The ones like Li-La, the ones the diplomats and scientists were talking to, they're the young. Adolescents. *Larvae.* No wonder they nip off to consult with the ancestors whenever things get a bit tricky.

There must be a point in their life cycle when some of them start processing hydrogen. Perhaps based on gender, or maybe they're fed royal jelly. Who knows?

Whatever it is, before they can become lift-cells they have to shed their juvenile vestiges. *That* is what they jettison as "dead weight". Like the husk a butterfly leaves behind, it is nothing to them and our requests that they treat their dead with more respect are nonsensical.

The adult cells travel between cities not as sky-taxis, but because *they're* the leaders, the elders, the ones with the knowledge and experience. It's communication, or communion.

And they can't provide samples, or swap tech, because there *is* no technology to share. It's all biology, all body chemistry. Somehow, the A-Gees can control their physical forms to do any number of tasks we'd have to build machines to do. Or maybe, like a jellyfish, they're not actually *one* species but many, living together for a common purpose.

Mr Franklin's biology lessons have come in handy after all. Because they've told me how *weird* life on earth is. And surely we have to expect alien life to be even weirder.

The aliens don't want to explain themselves to us because we couldn't possibly understand.

All they want is for us not to worry. All they want is to be left alone.

I wonder what happens after the A-Gees have lowered the methane and CO_2? When we're not so dependent on each other. Will we still be able to coexist peacefully?

I sincerely hope so. It was beautiful up there. Sometimes I dream of flying. I suppose we all do. Only now I actually think of it, it was never flying—it was floating.

Before I leave, I take one last look up at the bright canopy above me. The roof of the cell I've been listening to contains a myriad of much smaller cells, some darker than others.

Are these... *baby* A-Gees? There's at least a hundred of them, maybe a thousand. No wonder the cloud-cities proliferate so fast.

No wonder the A-Gees are peaceful. Or probably, *hopefully* so. When every wall, every staircase is sentient, any weapons would be completely unlike anything we use. No guns, knives, or explosives. If they have anything at all, I bet we have no defence against them, just as A-Gees would have no defence against tracer fire and air to air missiles.

If we ever fought we'd end up waging totally different wars, winning one, losing the other.

Best not go there.

These thoughts keep me subdued as Li-La guides me down. The meeting below is coming to an end, the helicopter on its way to pick us up. From the grim faces of the politicians, little if anything was resolved.

But that's *okay*, I think. Whatever the A-Gees do, we'll just have to get used to them.

We've gotten used to far worse.

I wonder if the Yrill know anyone who could clean up our oceans?

"Lighter than Air" originally appeared in *Gotta Wear Eclipse Glasses* on 1 June 2020.

About the author

Liam Hogan is an award winning short story writer, with stories in *Best of British Science Fiction 2016* and *2019*, and *Best of British Fantasy 2018* (NewCon Press). He's been published by *Analog, Daily Science Fiction*, and *Flame Tree Press*, among others. He helps host Liars' League London, volunteers at the creative writing charity Ministry of Stories, and lives and avoids work in London. More details at happyendingnotguaranteed.blogspot.co.uk, @LiamJHogan

Regret's Relief

Travis Wade Beaty

I would have never gone to the Glyphs of Onyx if I hadn't fallen in love. I was in my final year at the University of Spell-Craft in Silver Forge. And as Silver Forge was the nearest port to the island of Onyx, and as the glyphs had been discovered only five years prior, students were always taking little holidays up there to see them. Most returned unimpressed. The Onyxian parliament itself had investigated the glyphs and not only had they concluded there was no magic to them, but also questioned whether they held any meaning whatsoever. Still, rumors persisted. And a few students, enough to be an annoyance, returned from Onyx as full converts. They would tell how the glyphs had imparted to them a special inspiration. And how they were certain, because of this special inspiration, that they were about to craft a monumental spell, one that could change the world.

As no such spell ever materialized, I was happy to focus on my studies and ignore all the hullaballoo. But then I met Celia.

In truth, I met her paintings first. I had gone down to the annual campus art show and found myself mesmerized by a set of mournful landscapes. Nothing about them suggested spell-craft. Nothing in them moved or twinkled or morphed into something new as you took them in. And yet, try as I might, I could not take my eyes off of the paintings until a deep sorrow rose within me and I wept. A woman approached and I hurried to wipe my eyes, embarrassed by my emotional outburst. When I turned to meet her eye, she gave a sympathetic smile.

"It's the damnedest thing," I said. "There's no spell on these paintings. They seem to belong in a mundane gallery."

"And yet?" she asked.

"And yet they've done something to me. As if something has been released that I didn't know was bottled up."

The woman nodded. "There's no spell cast on the painting because the painting is the spell," she said. "You spell-writers don't cast spells on top of the incantations you write, do you?"

I had never considered such an idea. All the spell-paintings I had ever seen were painted with the idea that certain incantations, usually ones that would animate the painting, would be cast on top.

"And what is the spell painted here?" I asked, pointing to the landscapes.

"I call it, 'Unearthing Sorrow'."

"That's genius," I said.

She smiled her true smile then, the one that lit up her face, the room, and, I was certain, the whole world. By some miracle, she took a fancy to me as well, and we fell under that kind of love spell which remains a mystery to cast; the one from which there is no cure but for one or both hearts to be torn asunder.

Our studies kept us busy in the day, but every evening we'd meet up to take long walks around the campus. During one of those moonlit strolls, Celia confessed that she had visited the glyphs in Onyx and felt the presence of her mother in the caves. She told me how, when she was still in her adolescence, her widowed mother had turned down a marriage proposal from a wealthy textile merchant. For years Celia had resented her for not wedding the merchant, blaming all the family's woes and poverty on her mother's pride. Until, finally, after the death of her younger sister from the crimson cough, Celia released a fit of rage on her mother, who had passed out of the world that very night.

"I have told myself a thousand times that my words didn't end her life," Celia said. "The fever did that. But I am always replaying those horrible last words I spoke to her. Standing next to the glyphs, I felt her presence. It was as if she were standing just behind the cave wall. And it seemed I had a chance to take those words back. I did and I told her —"

Her words caught in her mouth and she cried. I realized why Celia's paintings had worked so well on me. We shared a similar grief.

"And you saw an apparition in the caves? You saw your mother?" I asked.

"I felt her," she said. "It was as if the caves were commiserating with my grief."

"And did she hear you?" I asked, my heart in my throat.

"I don't know. But it helped to say the words out loud. To … allow them. I can't explain it. You have to go, Ben. You have to know them for yourself."

So, late in the summer, I boarded a zeppelin and floated over the North Sea to a shore of stark white sand and craggy black rock. Beyond the shore, a city rose, culminating in the gleaming white dome of the Onyxian Parliament sitting high on a hill.

I dropped my bag off at a ramshackle inn next to the southern docks and set off for the glyphs. They were not hard to find, as there was a steady stream of tourists heading to and from them. I followed the crowd down a winding path that ran along the cliffs facing the shore. Eventually, the path veered left and sloped down into the wide entrance of a cave. I had to brace myself as a strong and constant ocean breeze rushed past me and down into the cool mouth of the cave.

There was no need for a lantern, as there were so many lantern-wielding tourists already inside. In less than a half an hour I had made my way to the glyphs, which were in a small chamber off the main path. They seemed no more than geological anomalies, odd-looking white striations set in a black cave wall. I held the palm of my hand against them, as I saw some other tourists doing, and felt nothing. I returned to my inn dismayed that I had not felt even the slightest fraction of magic. But that night, I had a dream. The dream. The one that had plagued me since I was a child.

It was always the same: the dream began with a cruel reenactment of the worst day of my life – the day I decided to read "Colonel Bellington's Compendium of Spell-forms" instead of watching over my younger brother, Arthur. I was twelve and he was a capable five years old, but my mother still insisted I go with him whenever he wanted to swim. I sat under an apple tree as he flew into the water, and lost myself in the compendium.

"Come play, Ben!" he yelled out, splashing in the water. "Novels are boring."

"It's not a novel," I said. "It's a compendium of spells."

"Is there a spell to make me a shark?"

"These aren't for casting. They're just examples."

"You should read how to do fun stuff! You should learn how to make mud puddles when there's no rain. Or a spell that can turn me into a shark."

I don't know what he said after that because I began to ignore him. I became lost in the book and didn't look up from the page until I heard my father's cries. He had come in from the fields to wash in the pond and found Arthur in the lily-pads, floating blue.

From there, the dream departed from true events. I would descend into the pond, not to save Arthur, but to speak to him, to beg his forgiveness. My words would float away, a stream of shining bubbles racing to the surface, while Arthur looked on, his face blank, his eyes dead. And this scene would play out for an eternity until I awoke.

That night in Onyx, my dream was so vivid that I awoke choking, the taste of pond water still in my mouth. I was uncomfortably hot, sweating even after pulling off the sheets of my bed. I put on my boots and stepped outside, but the slight breeze coming off the shore gave no relief. I heard a chirp from above and looked to see a cloud of bats, their black wings barely visible against the midnight sky. They dove into the cliffs and I knew they must be following that chill current of wind that never stopped flowing into the caves. I had to join them, to find cool respite in the womb of the earth, and I hurried toward the caves, certain they were the only cure for my fever.

Still in my night clothes, with only the light of my single lantern, I descended into the caverns as the wind whipped around me. I felt a strange joy, as if being welcomed home after a long voyage, and could not keep myself from smiling. The caves should have been impossible to navigate in so little light, but I could not seem to take a wrong step. I somehow knew my way as if I were in my childhood home. When I came to the glyphs, my fever broke and a chill went through me. I had an odd sensation that Arthur was in the cave somewhere nearby. I spoke his name and waited for an answer.

A sudden gust of wind caught me off guard and I lost my balance. I dropped my lantern as I fell and, with a loud clang, all went black. At first, the darkness of the cave was nothing but a void, but as I scrambled to find my lantern, shapes began to fill in the void. There was an apple tree and below it a familiar book with a red cover. Beyond, I saw lush green grasses growing tall around a wide pond. Arthur came storming out of the water, his lanky limbs glittering in the afternoon sun. His mouth moved as if he were speaking but I couldn't hear him.

"Arthur!" I yelled and scrambled to my feet.

Urgently, he pointed behind me. I turned to see the red book beneath the apple tree flying toward me. It hovered in the air before me and opened itself. Its pages were blank, but as I peered into the book, a spell began to write itself. My heart swelled as I felt this must be a spell made especially for me, a spell that would allow me to speak with my brother, to finally beg his forgiveness and bring peace to both our hearts. I tried to read what was written but it was all in gibberish. I turn back to Arthur and saw a vast canyon of darkness had fallen between us.

"I'm sorry!" I yelled out. "I'm sorry! Can you hear me?"

But as I spoke, he dissolved into the darkness. I ran forward to find him as if there were a great stretch of space ahead of me and not a wall of stone. My head slammed against the hard rock and it felt as if I'd been sucker-punched by a prizefighter. I dropped to the ground and held my throbbing head until the pain dulled. As I did, the cave winds started back up and I could not stop shivering.

"Please," I said. "Please come back."

"Gotta come in the spring," a voice said. There was a flicker of yellow light and I made out a puffy-faced man sitting on the floor of the cave, his back against the glyph wall. He was holding a match and using it to light my lantern. He glared at me with hollow eyes, made a move to get up, decided he was too drunk for that and leaned once more against the wall.

"In the spring," he spat out. "Hasn't anybody told you! They ain't at their full power until the spring, dammit."

"Who are you?" I asked.

"That's not important. What the glyphs say, that's what's important. That's all that matters, isn't it?" he said "But you fools keep coming at the wrong time. Say it, then. You'll come back in the spring."

"I'll come back in the spring," I said.

"Good man. Now leave," He said thrusting the lantern into my hand. When I hesitated he yelled out "Get the hell out of here!"

He grew angrier, shouting various profanities until I fled back up to the surface. I was sure he was mad, but at the moment, madness made a great deal of sense. I took his advice to heart and promised myself to return in the spring.

On the zeppelin flight home, as I floated further from the glyphs, I could only think of Arthur in the caves and how he had nearly spoken to me. I decided I would devote my life to deciphering the spell I had not been able to read in that floating red book, that no matter how impossible a task it seemed, I would devise a spell to speak with the dead.

I returned to Silver Forge brimming with faith and optimism, happy to join the ranks of the true-believers. I asked Celia if she would go to Onyx with me once we had our degrees.

"Is this a proposal?" she asked.

"Dammitall, I think it is," I said.

I had no ring to present, but she didn't mind. She painted thin black bands on each of our ring fingers, and, together, we cast a spell to make the ink permanent. We graduated in the fall, exchanged vows, slid silver rings over our painted ones, and promptly sailed to Onyx.

The strangest thing about the island was not the spell crafting or the seclusion or even the odd political corruption of a city whose main export was sorcery, but the fact that so many tolerated the torment of its winter. In the dead of an Onyx winter, you despised yourself for staying, but you couldn't get out. By then, hardly any boat would chance the ice surrounding the island, nor any zeppelin take on the near-constant storms.

Each autumn, when the frigid winds began to blow, most of the island's residents would take the last ferries of the season back to the mainland, and of course, the rich would book flights to the sunny beaches of Zephyr's Banks. But Celia and I, along with all the other artists, would stay.

We stayed because only an Onyx winter could make you fully know its spring. Come visit with the tourists in the warm months and you would write home about how beautiful it was. "Oh, cousin Meredith, you must come to see the sparkling white beaches. And the old prince's castle on the precipice by moonlight. And the tulips blooming in all the colors of the rainbow!"

All fine and well, but if you wanted to know why the artists were here, you had to survive the winter. Then, when spring finally emerged, you would know her properly as your savior. Born again, you would kiss her feet, joyous to be swallowed in her ever-blooming ecstasy. And in this state you would have your best chance with the glyphs.

In the midst of that first winter, with frost on our breath even as a fire roared in our hearth, Celia and I decided we'd leave Onyx before another one came to pass. But in the spring, we went down into the caves, set our hands on the glyphs, and returned to the surface with our minds abuzz with inspiration. We strolled through the hills of blooming wildflowers as sand swirled on the beaches and waves lazily collapsed on the shore and we agreed we'd live in Onyx all the days of our lives.

When I had laid my hands on the glyphs that first spring I did not see Arthur, but heard his voice in my head, faintly humming his favorite lullaby. All the lyrics came back to me and it occurred to me they could be turned into a stellar sleeping spell. I decided this must be the first step in devising a spell to speak with the dead. I would combine an intense sleeping spell with one that could summon the deceased. And in this way, I would bring the living closer to death while luring the deceased closer to life. And there in the space between worlds, the living and the dead could commune. Did it bother me that I had no idea how to cast a spell on the deceased? That there was no precedent for it whatsoever? Not in the least. Standing before the glyphs, I had faith the details would iron themselves out. But when I sat down at home to begin writing, all my ideas became confused and impossible. What seemed rational in the caves, was absurdity anywhere else.

Meanwhile, Celia had felt moved to honor her mother and began a painting of her childhood home. She played with light in a new way and the painting was like a breath of fresh air for the soul. For a time, it was a joy to have that painting in our home, but Celia was never satisfied with it. She could not leave it alone. She painted over her work many times as spring became summer until the composition became disjointed and the only feeling it conjured was confusion.

We spent five years that way, cursing the winters, exalting the springs, and spending the months in between telling ourselves our big break-through was just around the corner.

I found work as a typesetter and Celia waited tables and we tried our best to make a name for ourselves as spell-crafters on an island teeming with people attempting to do exactly the same.

We had some mild successes. I had a knack for writing tawdry love spells which I published under a pen name. Most of them were dirt cheap, wore off too quickly, and had dubious effects, but love spells were in such demand, they could always sell. Celia would go down to the boardwalk and sell paintings to tourists of stars that would actually twinkle in night skies and suns that set before your very eyes. It was enough to keep us at our craft, but not enough to pay the bills.

By the fifth year, up to our necks in debt and without a break in sight, Celia made her case that we ought to leave.

"I'm stuck, Ben," she said. "It doesn't matter if I paint a carnival or a funeral. All my paintings are about my mother. I thought moving here, feeling my mother in the caves, would help me heal, but it's only made me fixated on her deathbed. I can't stand it anymore."

I had to admit that we were spinning our wheels, and wondered if the glyphs had ever been on our side. I began to think perhaps it was all some kind of cosmic joke and the caves were feeding off our frustrations. I could still sense Arthur when I stood before the glyphs, but I never had a vision as intense as my first trip. And despite a great deal of study, I had come no closer to writing a spell to speak with the dead. I asked Celia for a few weeks to mull over the idea of leaving the island for good. And while I did, winter came early. It came hard, choking the streets in snow and ice. The whole city shut down for months. Celia and I spent a great deal of time huddled by our fire, talking over the future. How we would move back to Silver Forge where the weather was mild, where rent was cheap and where spell-crafters like us could easily find work tutoring students. And then one morning I woke with a fever, retching from the taste of pond water in my mouth.

"Ben, don't be a moron," Celia said when she saw me putting on my boots. "There's still snow on the ground." Her auburn hair was pulled back and her smock was splattered in violet specks of paint. She had woken early and had begun painting before we'd even made coffee.

I put two layers of sweaters on and said, "There's been a shift. Spring is here. I've never felt it so strong. You feel it too, don't you?"

"I did feel it," she said. "I woke inspired." She sighed and wiped her forehead, smearing purple paint across it. "I had a vision of hope."

I examined her painting. It was the landscape just outside our window. There were the city rooftops, all in shadow, and beyond, the low rolling hills covered in snow. Above the hills, Celia had painted a lone seagull. I thought he might drop out of the pale blue sky at any moment out of sheer despair.

"How do you feel?" she asked.

"Heavy," I said.

She slammed her paintbrush down on the easel. "I give up," she said. "I can't escape my mother, or rather, my insufferable self-pity. I'm a one-trick pony. It's all despair and grief and sorrow and blah, blah, blah."

She turned to me, hands on her hips. "I think we ought to make a child."

"Right now?"

"Yes, please."

"You'd have a child as if you were casting a spell. As if there's some magic in it that will make you stop painting your mother."

She shrugged. "Why wouldn't it?"

I laughed. "Be serious. We can barely feed ourselves, Cee-Cee!"

"We're moving, remember? To a place where people like us are sought after. Where we aren't just another set of dreamers."

"Let's not put the cart before the horse. We'll move and then make a family."

I put on my cloak and poured what was left of the previous night's broth into a canteen.

"Where are you going?" she asked. "There's no way the shops are opening this early. I don't care how much we feel it's spring."

"I'm going to the glyphs."

"Moron! You'll slip on some black ice in those caves and that'll be the end of you."

"I have to go."

"Why?"

"Arthur told me."

Just before I awoke that morning Arthur had finally done something besides stare at me with his wretched dead eyes. When I had descended into the pond, he had turned to look behind him. There, instead of the usual sun-streaked murk of the pond, I had seen the glyphs, shining bright in the darkness.

Having heard this explanation, Celia turned to her painting and sighed. She addressed the canvas as if it were an old friend familiar with my nonsense.

"I can't argue with Arthur, can I?" she asked.

"I'm sorry," I said.

"Go then, moron. I very much hope you don't die."

I trudged through the snow toward what I thought should be the entrance of the caves, but the cliffs were still blanketed in snow. I sipped my broth and waited for the sun to rise. As it did, the snows shrank and little streams of icy water began to race toward the shores. Finally, a mass of snow toppled from the cliffs and, beyond it, I made out the dark maw of the cave entrance.

I lit my lantern and descended into the cave, but when I reached the entrance to the glyph chamber, I paused. Something was off. I stood a long while contemplating what it was until I realized there was no wind in the cave. And in the place of the rushing wind I could hear a low hum, a vibration I could feel in my bones. I had the distinct feeling there was someone waiting for me. I thought for sure I'd find that old drunk man sitting against the glyph wall, but when I stepped forward, I was alone.

As soon as I saw the glyphs, they began to move. They shifted, blurred, and melted into the cave wall. I was horrified that they might vanish for good. I tried to run to them, but darkness enveloped me. I flailed my arms and realized I was under water, floating in the pond behind my childhood home. I turned my head and there was Arthur, floating before me, only he was alive. I knew he was alive. And I knew I could reach out and bring him back. I knew we'd climb a tree and race for the highest branch. We'd catch frogs and drop them at the top of the hill so we could chase them back down into the pond. And we'd laugh at how he'd almost drowned.

I reached and pulled him to me, and as I did, I was pulled once more into myself. Alone, I stood in the cave, submerged not in water, but in a torrent of thought.

I had a clarity of mind like I'd never experienced before, or since. Parts of spells I had been mulling over for months began sliding into one another and making themselves whole. I sprinted out of the cave in a ruckus and burst forth into the sunlight surrounded by a cloud of black wings that screeched and fluttered into the pink evening sky.

"I have it!" I yelled. "I have it all!"

When I stormed through the door of our flat, I saw that Celia had destroyed the painting she'd been working on. It had been doused in scarab ether, a highly effective paint thinner. All the colors had melded together into a sick dripping brown. Celia was passed out in bed, her smock still on, our last bottle of wine lying empty in her arms. The myriad of burning thoughts shooting through my mind all fell away. The sight of Celia in such disarray stripped me of any other idea than to relieve her of her grief. Celia was the kindest, warmest person I knew, and it seemed a great injustice that she ought to carry the guilt of her mother's deathbed with her always.

Barely thinking, I sat down and wrote "Regret's Relief" for her. The spell allowed a person to forgive themselves, irrevocably, for what they most regretted. I had such a clarity of thought it was not hard to make scarab ether the only casting cost, and as soon as it was written, I cast "Regret" on my still sleeping Celia. I then turned back to my desk and began to write the spell that I felt was my destiny. A spell to speak with the dead.

I started off well enough, but halfway through, my writing became confused. I read over my work several times, trying to regain my train of thought until my eyelids grew heavy. Exhaustion overwhelmed me and I passed out on my writing table. I awoke shivering, the fire in our flat having gone out. I read the partially finished spell and it seemed as foreign as if another hand had written it. The clarity of the glyphs had fogged over.

The inspiration did not return, even when I went back down into the caves. It was as if the glyphs had given me the totality of their gift and the tap was now shut off. Still, every morning I would wake and force myself to attempt finishing the spell. Each morning would end with me pounding my fist on the writing table and burning all my failed work in the fire.

While my frustrations grew, Celia's abated. It took some time to see a change, and it was hard to say when exactly it took hold, but one day I knew it like I knew winter from spring. Her step was ever so faintly lighter, her sleep just a smidge deeper, and her smile, though I previously thought it impossible, became even brighter. Still, I watched her work closely. I had worried "Regret" would make her art suffer, that if she did not carry that certain pain, she couldn't infuse it into her art. And yet, the opposite was true. She now painted with more confidence and with a greater sense of purpose. Her grief was still there, but instead of wrestling with it, she embraced it and held it firm in her grasp.

People began swearing up and down that they felt an improvement in their health after visiting her exhibition. She leaned into this idea and found herself painting a sunrise that could ease a headache. All of Onyx came to see it. High Society took notice and began an onslaught of commissions she couldn't hope to keep up with.

By late spring, when parliament opened its door to the public, I was certain "Regret" had worked just as I had written it. I applied for patent approval and was immediately asked to present myself for questioning. Most of the patent committee agreed there had to be some sort of catch. That no spell, especially one that dealt with matters of the heart and mind, no matter how inspired, could be written that clean. I pointed out the spell could only be used once on each person, and they began to warm to its poetry. To test it, the head magistrate used the spell on herself. She wept, stamped my patent, left Onyx that very day, and never returned.

"Regret's Relief" was, however, deemed a protected spell that could not be sold to the public. Parliament feared the spell would be ill-used by the morally bankrupt, allowing degenerates to alleviate the weight of their conscience. Parliament would administer the spell only to those who seemed fit after thorough interviews. I agreed to their terms and received a lump sum of 500 dollars.

I paid off our outstanding debts and bought the finest pen and paper money could buy. I told myself I could finish "Commune with the Dead" if only my hand could glide more smoothly across the page. I never wrote so much trash in all my life as with that damned pen. Occasionally I'd stumble upon a functional spell, but nothing close to finishing "Commune." The best I crafted was an incantation to make mourners more talkative at their loved one's wake.

I also had to deny my constant urge to seek out the glyphs, allowing myself to descend only once per week. And though they never gave me a single clue on how to finish "Commune", I kept going until, at the peak of summer, the caves were shut down. When I arrived that afternoon, police guarded the entrance. I joined the other agitated glyph devotees as tempers flared until the coroner arrived and announced there had been a death in the caves. I stayed to watch the government spelunkers haul a body out and saw that it was the old drunk man from my first visit to the caves. Someone in the crowd wondered if he'd drunk himself to death.

"Glyph-sickness!" a woman yelled out. "They won't write that in the obituary, but it's the truth. Seen it too many times! Sonovabitch had a family and everything."

On my walk home I had to stop as my stomach clenched. I doubled over and vomited my lunch onto the grass. As I convulsed, I realized I resented the old drunk, then I despised him, and then I hated him with all my being. The bastard was more than half the reason I'd come to Onyx in the first place and now he was keeping me from my glyphs, keeping me from "Commune with the Dead", keeping me from Arthur. I thought I might have strangled the son of a bitch if he weren't already dead.

I returned home sweating and belligerent, to find Celia painting furiously. Our flat was covered with her finished work, every painting a sunrise, every one heartbreakingly beautiful. My temper cooled as I took in the landscapes and I wondered at how I could have been so angry about the death of a stranger.

Celia rushed to me, slapping zeppelin tickets in one hand and a glass of bubbly in the other. The tickets were for Zephyr's Bank.

"How much did this cost?" I asked.

"The Dome, Ben! I'm in the Dome!"

She had won a showing at the Obsidian Dome, at the time the most prestigious gallery in the hemisphere.

To celebrate, she demanded we go on vacation. As it turned out, she'd been stowing cash in secret to surprise me. She insisted we go all out and rent a cottage on Zephyr's Bank. As there seemed no option to disagree, I told myself it was providence. I could take a break from the glyphs, and perhaps gain a new perspective on "Commune with the Dead."

It was while we were in Zephyr's Bank that the Patent Committee of the Onyxian Parliament let "Regret's Relief" be known to the public, writing at length about its potentials in The Northwestern Journal of Incantation. Word spread through Zephyr quickly until Celia came to dinner with her eyes brimming over with tears.

"Ben," she said, "did you cast it on me?" The truth of it was so plain, I couldn't hope to lie. I confessed. She held me and cried and thanked me. I apologized for casting the spell on her without her consent. She said she didn't care. And then she pled for me to cast it on myself.

"It wouldn't work the same," I said. "I have too many regrets."

"Look at you. Every night I hear you gasping and groaning. You haven't had an honest night's sleep in months. And your days are spent working on this cursed spell that clearly doesn't want to be written. This has to stop, Ben."

Leaving Onyx had not, as I'd hoped, alleviated my desire for the glyphs. I woke several times each night, always in a sweat and gasping for air. I would spend most of my days sitting on the beach with my journal and pen, facing the direction of Onyx, sometimes writing, but mostly staring out at the sea. In the face of insurmountable evidence against my mental well-being, I had no choice but to lie.

"I'm fine," I said. "Creating a spell so immense has put me in a state of unrest, but there will be an end."

The lie sounded good and I decided to believe it myself. "Every day," I said, "I come closer to finishing my work."

"Then let's make a child," Celia said. "What are we waiting for? Poverty is no longer an excuse. People will throw money at you and me alike, just to hear us pontificate on the arts."

"We're on our way up, Celia. Children would only slow us down."

"I want a child, Ben."

"Soon."

"Why not now?"

"Let art be your child!"

She struck me then. Celia, who barely had the nerve to smack a gnat, made the full brunt of her painter's hand known to me.

"Don't make this about me," she said. "It's about you. It's about Arthur."

We did not speak the rest of that day, nor the next, which was our final day of the vacation. We did, however, follow through on our plan to picnic for dinner. We had yet to observe the evening ritual of the crabs coming into the bay, and neither of us wanted to miss it. We sat on the beach in silence as the crab's mating ritual set the night shore aglow in a humming violet bioluminescence. The full moon hung low, shining bright. It pulled at the womb of the earth and I felt that gravity shoot through my soul. For a fleeting moment, I saw myself making a family with Celia. She must have seen it in my eye because she said, "I deserve it, Ben. We deserve it."

She was lying on the bed of bluegrass, just off the sand, in an ivory gown bathed in starlight. The King of Fairies might have mistaken her for his queen. I played the part of an ass and did nothing about it. Instead, I looked out over the bay, and even though I knew it was impossible, I decided I could see the shores of Onyx on the horizon.

In the morning, as I was packing my things for the return, Celia laid her hand on mine.

"Let's stay," she said.

I froze and waited for her to go on, but she only stared at me steadfast and pitying.

"I have to return," I said.

"That island is making you sick, Ben. We should be the happiest we've ever been, but you're a mess. My sister is a day's train ride away in Silver Forge. Let's go for a visit."

I allowed myself to consider not returning to Onyx and my stomach turned itself over. Bile rose in my throat.

"This is how you repay me?" I asked. "I release you from the torment of your mother and now you'd stop me from writing my masterpiece?"

"I'm going to Silver Forge," she said. "And I want you to come with me. What I'm not going to do is watch you torture yourself when you could simply cast 'Regret' on yourself and be free from Arthur."

"You mean I should leave him behind. Abandon him."

"He's gone, Ben."

"Go, then. Go to Silver Forge and find some poor schmuck and make all the babies you want."

She didn't dignify my attack with a response. She only packed her things, told me to come to Silver Forge when I was ready, and left on the next train. I told myself it was all for the best. That our paths had diverged. We were getting in the way of each other's happiness.

When I returned to Onyx I marched straight for the caves, only to find the entrance still boarded over. Only now there was a notice glued to the boards announcing that another poor soul had died in the caves and, until thorough investigations could be completed, the caves were closed indefinitely.

Celia wrote asking me to send her painting supplies, and a few weeks later, she wrote again asking for her wardrobe. Several months after that, she asked for the rest of her things. In each letter she would describe the many well-paying jobs I could take on in Silver Forge and how she thought she could set up her own school for spell-painting. I shipped her things off and responded to her letters by repeating the lie I now held most dear: that I was oh so very close to finishing my work and that I would be along soon.

Eventually, the flat was void of most all her things and I realized how little I had. There was my writing table, the bed, the dresser of clothes. They all stared at me like idiot friends.

"All for the best," they said. "Now you're free to get some real work done."

Winter came and I spent it alone in a flat that was too empty and in dreams that were too real. There were a few dark days in the dead of winter where I convinced myself the flat was the afterlife, a purgatory made up special for me.

When spring returned and I was able to go out and meet with people again, I gained back some sanity. I wrote a letter to Celia telling her I was ready to have children. That I was going to write a book of love spells. That I was done with the glyphs and "Commune with the Dead" for good. I took it to the post office and was about to drop it into the mail bin when a vision came to me. I saw a host of my own children perishing as they fell off of roofs, tripped down stairs, got run over by trains, and drowned in ponds while I sat hunched over my writing desk. I took the letter home and fed it to the fire.

I began taking sleeping draughts to keep my dreams at bay and quickly became addicted to them. When those became too expensive, I turned to hard liquor. I lost my typesetting job and was booted from the flat after missing half a year's rent. I washed dishes for The Mermaid's Tale and the owner let me stay in his attic. I told myself I was waiting for a sign from the glyphs, or Arthur, or something I could not name.

When the ferries once more declared they had two weeks left before they closed for the winter, I wept. I was a failure, and a drunk to boot. I felt myself a coward as well, terrified of another winter in Onyx, of what it might do to my mind. I bought a ferry ticket for Silver Forge. I had an idea I would search out Celia and beg her forgiveness, but as the ship left the dock, I rushed off, leaping back to the shore.

"Now," I told myself. "Now that you've given up all you have. Now that you've shown the glyphs how serious you are, they will deliver you!"

I stumbled through the first snow flurries of the year, my veins coursing with more booze than blood. I brought a hammer with me and the last I remember was many failed attempts to pry the boards off the cave entrance.

When I came to, I was lying on a hospital bed. Celia stood over me. Her belly was round with child and her hair was shorter but shone brighter. She had dark circles under her eyes and I could tell that she had been crying.

"Dammitall," I said. "You've got to leave. I don't want you to see me like this."

"Too late," she said, and she laid her hand on mine. I saw her silver wedding band was gone, but the one of black ink remained.

"You shouldn't be here," I said. "Winter will come. You'll be stranded."

"You're right," she said. "I have tickets to return to Silver Forge tomorrow morning. So buck up and show these nurses you can walk out of here."

I found I could stand on my own, and I put on my best show for the nurses. Celia signed me out of the hospital and escorted me down to Angler's Brewery by the piers. She had sold a painting to the owner recently and wanted me to see it. So we sat by the Angler's hearth and took in her work, hung over the mantel.

The painting was of our flat, back when we'd both inhabited it. I waited until the cordial I'd ordered was finished before I took my eyes off the painting and steadied them on Celia.

"I feel no change," I said. "I fear your painting's a dud."

"I think you should write some spells for Arthur."

"That's what I've been trying to do."

"No. You've been trying to write something for yourself. Write something for Arthur."

I could see she was watching me, the way I had once watched her. I looked at the painting again and a weight lifted. A key turned. A frost on my heart shook free.

She laughed and wept at the same time. "I'm sorry it took so long to paint. You're a stubborn little moron, so it had to be just so."

"What is it? Did you somehow paint 'Regret's Relief?'"

"No. I went with a different approach."

"What then?"

She smiled. "A love spell."

"And whom will I fall in love with?"

"Yourself. You'll love yourself as much as I did. As much as I do. And there's nothing you can do about it, moron."

She sat back in her chair, arms crossed, beaming.

I thought of saying "Damn you to hell," but all that came out was, "Thank you, Celia."

She wiped her eyes, took a deep breath, and stared at the ring of ink on her left hand.

"Help me cast this off?" she asked.

"Maybe I won't."

"You will."

"Why?"

"Because you love me."

We spoke the spell together and I watched as the ink slowly faded away from both our hands.

We shared one glass of wine and I let her go home. I sat in Angler's, ordered a coffee, paper, and an ink-pot. I scribbled out a spell I called "Puddle Prisms" that made mud puddles that shone with all the colors of the rainbow. I used all my knowledge of shadows and light to make an illusion wherein ordinary fish would momentarily look like great big sharks. And then I wrote another spell for Arthur, and another, and as I wrote I felt Arthur's spirit rise within me and go swimming across the page.

"Regret's Relief" originally appeared in *Metaphorosis*
on 8 May 2020.

About the author

Travis Wade Beaty grew up in Northern Indiana, spent a good deal of his twenties in Los Angeles, and now resides in Washington, DC. While he's had a great many jobs, his favorites have included acting, teaching, and being a stay-at-home dad to two girls and three cats.

traviswadebeaty.wordpress.com, @TravisWBeaty

Old News

Gustavo Bondoni

"It just isn't fair," Sofia said.

"What isn't?" her grandmother replied absently from the kitchen. She took care of Sofia every other Saturday, while her parents worked.

"These people, they want their land back."

The sounds of cooking stopped and footsteps approached. Her grandmother glanced at the television. A noontime news program was on, transmitting live from Patagonia. "Many things in life aren't fair. If they get their land back, what will happen to the people who live there now? A lot of people live on that land today. Rich people, poor people, some of them have nowhere else to go."

Sofia thought about that. What her grandmother said made sense, of course. "I just wish there was some way I could help."

"There are many people who could use some help, Sofi."

"I would help them all, if I could, Abu."

Her grandmother looked down at her, eyes bright, but she said nothing.

On Sofia's 12th birthday, her grandmother pulled her aside, out of sight of her parents.

"What's up, Abu?" Sofia asked. She was pert and pretty in her brand-new yellow dress, and her mother had allowed her to dye the ends of her hair green.

Her grandmother looked at her sternly.

"If you had the power to change the world magically, what would you do?"

Sofia hesitated. There were so many things. But something she'd seen that morning on an Instagram post jumped out at her. "I would feed those little kids. You know, the ones in the camp in Italy. They can't go back home because of the war."

Her grandmother nodded curtly, once, and then her habitual smile returned.

The following Saturday, Abu sat her down and placed a piece of paper in front of her.

"Read it."

Abu's writing was nearly impossible for Sofi to decipher but she made the effort: "I, Sofia Viviani, will only use my magic to help those who truly need it." It was puzzling. "What is this? What magic?"

"It's a promise. You have to sign it." Abu held out an old fountain pen, old and made of metal, not the cheap plastic used by school children. "You have to sign it with this."

"Why?"

"Because if you sign it with this, it will become real. The pen is magical. What you write with it happens in real life."

Sofia studied the older woman's face, but there was no trace of humor in her expression, so she thought about it long and hard. "Give me the pen."

Abu watched her put down her name and then shook her head when Sofi tried to hand the pen back. "No. It's yours now. Be wise."

Sofía didn't help children in Italy. Not at first, anyway. She got distracted by the protestors on the news again. Tehuelche people were out on the streets of Bariloche, Argentina's most important mountain resort town.

It was, the news reported, the largest concentration of Tehuelche people in the century and a half. She was shocked to see how few of them there were, perhaps two hundred, all told.

"It's not right," she said.

It took her nearly two weeks to decide to take the pen to school, and when she did, she felt stupid for having brought it along. She suspected it was gold, and if she lost it she would be in real trouble. And, now that she thought of it, the mere idea of a magic pen felt incredibly silly.

So the day wore on and the pen remained in her bag. At 4:03 PM, just two minutes before the bell dismissed them for the day, she pulled it out and rushed a quick sentence: *Palermo Day School's seventh graders will be on a field trip to the Museo Sarmiento tomorrow (Friday).* Then she hid it beneath her desk, hoping no one had seen her. When the bell rang, she forgot all about it.

Until the next day. The teachers formed them up and led them into buses. Their destination? The Museo Sarmiento, where the Tratado Chegüelcho, the first treaty between the Patagonian tribes and European settlers, was on permanent display.

Too shocked to believe it wasn't all a crazy coincidence, Sofia still hedged her bets. She wrote: *The treaty will not be under glass, and I'll be able to write on it without anyone seeing me.*

To her shock, this, too, worked.

It wasn't easy. Bringing herself to deface a document of priceless historic significance was nearly impossible.

But she needed the wording. She needed the names. She couldn't build something like this herself: her attempts to do good would wreak havoc. She knew enough to know that.

The problem was that was pretty much all she knew. What would happen to the people there now? What were the natives even claiming? She was woefully underinformed.

Sofia stood before the document, smelling the ancient paper, and trying to read the script. One line jumped out at her: it spoke of land to the south of a river.

Not knowing what else to do, feeling the clock ticking, scared of being discovered, nearly crying in frustration, she reached out a trembling hand and scratched out the line after that one, replacing it with: *everyone involved will use the land as much as they truly need, and not more than that.*

Then she ran away.

Sofia brooded on the bus ride back from the museum, ignoring her friends. Had she changed anything, or would the museum discover the vandalism and come after her?

The afternoon passed in abject terror, fear of being called to the principal's office, expelled. Could they send a twelve-year-old to jail?

What had she been thinking?

The final recess of the afternoon found her hiding in the library, the one place where they would never look for her.

As the fifteen eternal minutes dragged, her eyes fell on the large map of South America on the wall. Strangeness penetrated the fog of her terror and she focused on it.

The familiar triangle that was Argentina was absent, replaced by three different-colored polygons. The northernmost was labelled Argentina and directly to the south was a green area was simply named the Eternal Peace Nature Reserve.

She was trying to make out the name of the southernmost portion when the bell rang.

"Abu," she said the next day. "I have a question."

"What is it?"

"Why give the pen to me? Why don't you help people yourself?"

"Ah, so you believe in it, now?"

"I think so."

Abu thought before speaking. "Each person has to use the pen in the way that suits them most. I helped our family. Not economically, but I made sure we led long, fulfilling lives... even if we're poor. When I realized that the world had bigger problems, it was too late for me to channel the magic differently. Believe me, I tried."

"I think I did something, but I'm not sure what."

"It works that way, sometimes. What happened?"

"The Nature Reserve. Eternal Peace. I think I had something to do with that."

"Sofi, the Reserve has been there for a century and a half. It's one of the greatest things ever done during the colonial era, a sudden attack of humanity in a brutal time. It's still used as an example of how things might be done when wise heads prevail." She shook her head. "I don't think you could have done much there."

"And the country to the south of that?"

"Jerun? What about it?"

"Is that where the Tehuelche live now?"

Her grandmother smiled. "Them and so many others; our best friends, our greatest allies. Since the treaty, we've worked together to maintain the Reserve. Everyone has benefitted. You'll learn all about it in high school. It must have been a great man who decided to word the treaty that way. Too bad historians can't agree on who it was."

"Oh." Sofia suddenly understood how it worked, the price she would pay. Loneliness would be her lot. "I hope I can do good things like that. Using the pen, I mean."

"Yes. That's a good guide." Her grandmother stroked her hair. "I knew you'd understand. That's why I chose you."

Sofia shivered. She understood more than her grandmother—or anyone else—would ever know.

"Old News" originally appeared in *Community of Magic Pens* on 4 May 2020.

About the author

Gustavo Bondoni is novelist and short story writer with over three hundred stories published in fifteen countries, in seven languages. He is a member of Codex and an Active Member of SFWA. His latest novel is *Test Site Horror* (2020). He has also published two other monster books: *Ice Station: Death* (2019) and *Jungle Lab Terror*(2020), three science fiction

novels: *Incursion* (2017), *Outside* (2017)   and *Siege* (2016)   and   an   ebook
novella   entitled *Branch*.   His   short   fiction   is   collected   in *Pale
Reflection* (2020), *Off the Beaten Path*(2019) *Tenth Orbit and Other Faraway
Places* (2010) and *Virtuoso and Other Stories* (2011). In 2019, Gustavo was
awarded second place in the Jim Baen Memorial Contest and in 2018 he
received a Judges Commendation (and second place) in The James White
Award. He was also a 2019 finalist in the Writers of the Future Contest. His
website is at www.gustavobondoni.com and his Twitter is @gbondoni

The Chorley

Rachel Ayers

Little Annamarie wore a mournful expression. "Mama," she said, "I can't find my Chorley." Chorley was a ragged stuffed elephant that the girl had had since she was two.

"Where did you leave it?" the Mama asked, the air of distraction hardened on her features. She had taken off the VR glasses that she customarily wore throughout the long hours of the day, and even the child could see that she was irritated by the interruption.

"If I knowed, I wouldn't be sad," the girl pointed out.

"Knew," Mama corrected.

Annamarie stamped her foot. "Mama, I need my Chorley."

Mama sighed and turned away from her desk. "Child, I'm very busy with a big project. If you need your toy right now, you'll have to look for it."

She went back to tinkering with the things on her worktable: an odd assortment of wires and pentacles and computer chips and silver. This was merely a ruse, but Mama did not want the child to consider that Annamarie herself was the true project of the day. The weird energy of the awful, ancient house had combined with the child's own latent gifts, attracting or creating a … thing. The thing came every night, and seemed to grow and fluctuate with the child's moods. It was intriguing, and unexpected, and Mama thought Annamarie might even have an early breakthrough, gaining a measure of control over her aura—most of the children in the Endeavor did not have any kind of control until they reached puberty. After weeks of monitoring it, she'd realized that the toy was somehow amplifying Annamarie's aural energies, and Mama decided that taking it would present the child with a fascinating new challenge.

It was not strictly prohibited in the Endeavor; side projects were allowed as long as they could be justified.

Annamarie spent a spare minute sulking before retreating in defeat; the Mama did not respond to this tactic.

Annamarie looked under her bed again, and in her closet. She was not, as a rule, a messy child, being rather precocious and having a strict Mama in the bargain. It was all the more mysterious that she couldn't find the toy, to which she had a deep attachment. She'd awakened from her nap to find it missing, and had looked all around their large and drafty house without a successful reunion with her lost Chorley.

At dinner Mama asked, "Did you look for your toy?"

"Yes, Mama." Annamarie was subdued.

Mama looked up from her soup and her newsscreen. "Did you find it?"

"No, Mama."

"Hmm. Well, I suppose you're too old for it, anyway."

This was grievously unfair, but Annamarie knew better than to remark upon it. Although she had an excellent vocabulary for a six-year-old, she could not explain to Mama that the stuffed toy had been painstakingly imbued with protective magic for the last four years, and that there were likely to be dire consequences if she were to retire to bed without it tonight. The spaces beneath the bed and within the wardrobe appeared to be perfectly mundane during daylight hours, but were in fact deep and dangerous repositories for the most nightmarish of creatures once darkness fell.

While she wanted to wail and kick her heels against the floor, Annamarie knew it would do no good; instead, she retreated to her bedroom. She looked around the familiar space, fighting the tears that threatened to fall down her plump cheeks.

She had a small desk, suitable to her short form, upon which she'd accumulated an assortment of electronic gadgets and loose ends from Mama's workshop, the yard, and the shadowy corners of the house. Annamarie had collected circuit boards since she liked the dark green shine of them, and countless wires, and other odds and ends, mostly gathered because of their interesting shapes.

There was a small, high window opposite the door, with a tattered pink curtain that hung limply over it. The curtain matched the quilt on the bed, and those two items were the beginning and end of any bright color in the room, except for, on a shelf over her bed, three other stuffed animals: a parrot, an anteater, and a jaguar. They had never held the special place in her heart which was reserved for the Chorley (named after the young elephant in the bedtime stories her Papa used to tell her).

She had two hours before bedtime, during which she was expected to study or, at the very most, quietly play. Mama was not supposed to be disturbed except during Meeting Times. Mama did not like other interruptions.

Annamarie pulled out her box of circuit boards, and a fistful of wires, and a small screwdriver she'd taken from the kitchen toolbox, and imitated the air of quiet contemplation Mama wore while she did her tinkering.

The girl frowned; she was missing something.

After a moment, she stood on her bed and pulled the other stuffed animals down to the floor with her. "I haven't knew you as long as my Chorley," she said quite solemnly, "but I still love you." She tapped her fingers against her lips, an uncommonly grown-up gesture. "I think you need to be boosted."

She selected a box-cutter—spirited away from Mama's worktable weeks ago—and ripped open the back of the jaguar without hesitation. Annamarie began to play intensely and with great purpose.

Mama, watching from the monitor, did not interrupt her child at bedtime. She was pleased and fascinated by this turn of events, which she had not anticipated, and she took notes for an hour, watching the child's selections and choices, enjoying the way the child mimicked her own work habits. The thaumo-meter hummed happily, measuring the surging energy around the child. Mama watched until the girl went to bed on her own initiative, the three newly modified stuffed animals arranged around her.

The thing that came in the night was perhaps more hungry than inherently evil, but still terrifying to little Annamarie. It oozed into the cracks created by darkness, nesting beneath the bed or curling in the closet. An unwary heel could be grabbed, tugged, and nibbled, if a dash to the bathroom was not properly executed.

The Chorley had protected her. The toy was alive with four years of devoted love; it was a powerful talisman against the thing, which was, after all, only acting according to its own nature. The Chorley repelled it, sent it scuttling for easier prey in other drafty houses. But now the Chorley was gone, and Annamarie had had to make do on short notice.

Mama straightened her glasses, ran her hands through her short-clipped hair, and turned on the dozen monitors which measured everything from the temperature of the room to the ectoplasmic content of the local atmosphere.

The other Mamas had much less to deal with. None of them had gotten stuck in a dark old house full of eaves and topped with crenellations—one variable too many, she'd argued, but been overruled—and most of the other Mamas still had their Papas around to help with their experiments. This Papa had gotten sentimental, protective of the innocent little girl, and that would not do. He'd been retired, peacefully enough. But then he'd tried to come back for Annamarie, and now Mama didn't know where he was, or if they'd even let him live.

She snorted to herself, turning off her computer screen and powering down her laptop for the night. She had a few hours of peace before the child woke. Annamarie was largely self-sufficient, but still required some persuasion in order to get her up and prepared to log in to her morning classes. Mama needed to sleep, but first she went through her own nightly ritual—which involved tea and a night light and a particular quilt, and which she never, ever would have admitted to performing to any of the other Mamas. She did not share anything with them beyond her notes on the child.

When Mama was fast asleep, and Annamarie tossed and turned beneath the surface of consciousness, the thing that came in the night began to ooze and creep into the girl's room. It had, as it always did, bypassed the lonely rooms of the house, and it moved by instinct away from the Mama's nightlight.

It slithered into the dark, cramped corner of the little girl's closet, watching her sleep. She was sweaty, muttering to herself and twitching—the best time, when it could invade the dreams and feed on the terror. An unwary foot was all well and good, but the thing that came in the night preferred fear to flesh. It liked to play with its food.

The child's talisman was gone: its bright blue glow, its glowering eyes, were not there to ward and guard the child. The thing that came in the night moved forward, undulating out of the closet, claws scraping into the cracks of the floorboards.

But it paused mid-rear before pouncing, studying the child on her bed more carefully. There was something wrong... something different.

The thing hissed, a slow angry boil of frustration and irritation.

Here were three new champions; and while they did not shine brightly, they cast their own faint glow through the room, and the edges of their light were painful to the thing that came in the night. They were nowhere near as strong as the Chorley, but they were vigilant, and there were three of them, and they were full of the love and playful energy of the child. Of course, Annamarie was extraordinary—or she would not have been chosen and taken for the Endeavor—and the toys were only one of the ways that her gift had manifested. That bright curiosity burned into something real, something that could affect the world in unexpected ways: it was exactly what the Mamas were trying to measure and control, with limited success. And now that power had been transferred into the toys, giving them a smaller measure of the child's aura, and granting her a sunny protection even as she slumbered.

The thing was forced to retreat, and it went, simmering with fury.

The Mama was unbearably smug during the conference call that took place during the early morning hours. She had every confidence that she understood the energies she'd measured.

"And she received no guidance from you on the matter?" the GrandMama asked.

"None at all," Mama assured her with a sniff. "She created three new guardians. All weaker than the one that's been soaking up her energy this whole time, but it was enough to get that... thing to leave her alone."

Another one of the Mamas spoke, hesitant. She was a new Mama, on her first child. "And you're certain that Annamarie doesn't suspect your part in any of this?"

"Of course not!" Mama said, though she did not really consider her answer before she said it. It had never even occurred to her as a possibility. Of course, the girl was precocious; all of the children were extraordinary. That was the whole point of the Endeavor. But they were still children, and Annamarie was only beginning to develop her talents.

"Keep a sharp eye on her," the GrandMama said. "The... thing is still a new development. We don't want your situation to go awry again."

The Mama schooled her face carefully, though she wanted to scowl. There had been no need to use that last word. This experiment was completely different, and Annamarie was far more talented than the last child the Mama had raised. It was hardly her fault that the last experiment had been abbreviated; of course, the child had died, so there was nothing that could be done about it except to move on. "I will certainly monitor the situation and present all my findings," she said. "On the child and the... thing."

She set aside her feelings of unease after the call. Certainly, there were more variables here than she had wanted, but she would work with what she was given, and she would be promoted within the Endeavor. If Annamarie lived, perhaps Mama could even move up with her. After all, she was the one who had thought of this experiment, and it looked like it might be just the emotional push the girl needed to advance her thaumatronics skills. If not with Annamarie, perhaps next time she could still begin with an older child, already aware of their aura; Mama had earned that much by now, surely. No more shepherding babies through their formative years. That would be a nice change.

For her part, when Annamarie woke, the girl was rested and relieved. The thing in the night had not gotten her, and her nightmares had been mild, even without her Chorley. She hugged her toys tightly in gratitude, and then got herself dressed and found breakfast and waited for Mama to log her into her class.

The toys were left to rest on the neatly-made bed, rather than the shelf above, and they were pleased with their change in status. It was not every day that a toy was elevated to best and beloved, and now that all three of them were now on the bed, well, they could not help but be pleased with themselves.

After her classes, and after Annamarie finished her walk—ten times around the yard, no more, no less—she took her nap with all three toys cuddled in her arms. None of them were particularly large, and with the modifications she'd made, they all had a few sharp edges and pokey bits. The girl didn't mind; she loved them all the more now that she'd made it through a night with them.

When she woke she had a little while before Meeting Time. Mama was busy in her office. She was very pleasant today, and had given Annamarie a cookie when she finished lessons. After her nap, Annamarie had an odd idea.

"Are you sure?" she asked the anteater, who seemed the wisest of the three.

The stuffed toy did not answer out loud, but Annamarie nodded reluctant understanding nonetheless.

Taking the jaguar under her elbow for courage, she crept out of her room, avoiding the creaking floorboards and slipping through Mama's bedroom door, opening it just shy of where it let out a long creaking groan. She rarely came in here; it was a cold room, always clean and tidy but never comfortable. Mama's bed was small, like her own, and although the room was much larger than Annamarie's, there was scarcely any more furniture in it.

Annamarie stopped, listening. She thought she heard a soft rustling from the darkness beneath the bed. She gripped the jaguar extra tight around the middle; the jaguar did not mind. Annamarie took comfort from his steady, stealthy presence, and edged around the room toward the closet.

This door let out a soft whine and Annamarie stopped with her head cocked, listening for Mama. She shivered and took one of the deep good breaths, and then she looked up on the top shelf of the closet.

There was her Chorley, carelessly flung so that it had toppled over on its side and lay on both of its own big, floppy ears. Annamarie let out a little sniffle at this pathetic sight. She reached her arms up, the jaguar still grasped by one ankle, and stood on tippy toes, but came nowhere close to reaching the stuffed elephant.

Annamarie left Mama's bedroom door propped open and crept back to her own room, sliding her bare feet along the rough floorboards where she knew they wouldn't creak. She gulped for air, back in her own room, and crushed the jaguar against her cheek for a final boost to her courage. Then she took the parrot and left her room again.

She paused outside Mama's office door; Mama was on the phone with someone, talking in one of the other languages. She was leaned back in her chair, with one arm over her eyes. While Annamarie watched, Mama straightened and lowered her arm, and her eyes brushed past the doorway where Annamarie stood.

But she didn't see Annamarie. She swiveled to face her desk, and Annamarie wrenched herself along.

She hovered uncertainly at Mama's closet door, looking at her Chorley. The one eye she could see—a scratched black button peeking over the edge of the shelf—implored Annamarie for rescue.

The little girl braced her feet evenly beneath her and tossed the parrot up toward the top of the closet. It was an impossible throw in the too-narrow space between the door and the shelf, and the elephant rested heavily and certainly on that shelf. Yet an instant later, both toys came tumbling back down and the girl caught them with no more than a muffled, feathery thump.

She heard a clunk and a clatter from Mama's office, and whirled around, clutching her toys. Another moment passed without a sound, and she tiptoed to the door, edging around Mama's dresser. When she passed the ugly little porcelain nightlight, the elephant's trunk snagged on the cord, and the thing tipped over with a *crunchthud*. The girl winced and froze. She set the light back upright, and fled to her own room. She did not tell Mama about the nightlight—Mama had taken her Chorley, after all, and could not be trusted—and there were no monitors in Mama's room, so, in later review, the other Mamas would never fully understand what happened that night.

When Mama came and got her for Meeting Time, the girl was on the floor, contentedly playing the coding game on her tablet. The parrot, anteater, and jaguar were ranged around her, as though they were participating in the programming.

"Make your bed more tidily tomorrow, Annamarie," Mama said. "It's very lumpy today."

"Yes, Mama," the girl said.

"Go and wash your hands and join me for supper," Mama said.

"Yes, Mama." She leapt up from the floor, grinning, but Mama had already started down the hall.

They ate a quiet dinner, and when they were done, Mama went back to her office and the girl went back to her room to do her homework.

When she went to bed that night, Mama was disgruntled to find that the bulb of her nightlight was not working. She gave a soft, muttered curse; she didn't have any spares. She'd have to get one tomorrow. Still, she was a grown woman, she reasoned. How much could a child's boogeyman really bother her?

At least she thought so, for a few more hours.

Annamarie slept blissfully well that night, with her modified toys ranged around her and the Chorley hugged tight in her arms. In the morning she woke late.

GrandMama was there. Annamarie did not like her. "Where's Mama?"

The old woman sniffed. "She's not... well. She won't be looking after you anymore."

"Will I get to see Papa?" A surge of excitement rippled through her.

"No," GrandMama said quickly. "No, you'll have a new Mama. I've come to take you to her." She glared around Annamarie's room; she found no fault with it, but still did not like the room... or the house, for that matter.

It took next to no time for Annamarie to dress and gather her things, hastily arranging her toys beneath her clothing. GrandMama recalled, uneasily, the Mama's report on how Annamarie had used her toys to channel her growing power... but with so many changes today, she would not take the toys from the child now. No, a smooth transition would be best; once everything else was under control, a new Mama could get the girl in line. GrandMama offered a hand, which the child reached to take, but a yucky jolt went through

Annamarie's arm. She pulled back to grip her suitcase instead.

"Are you ready, then, child?" GrandMama asked.

Annamarie nodded. Mama had always told her that she had to obey GrandMama, but Mama had taken her Chorley. Annamarie made a secret promise to her Chorley that she would not trust GrandMama, not ever. Or the new Mama either. Annamarie walked down the steps after GrandMama: suitcase dragging behind her, and, tucked carefully into the bag over her shoulder, her Chorley.

"The Chorley" originally appeared in *Metaphorosis*
on 31 July 2020.

About the author

Rachel Ayers lives in Alaska, where she writes and hosts shows for Sweet Cheeks Cabaret, daydreams, and looks at mountains a lot. She has a degree in Library and Information Science, which comes in handy at odd hours, and she obsesses over fairy tales and shares speculative poetry and flash fiction (and cat pictures) at patreon.com/richlayers.

richlayers.net, @richlayers

The Dinosaur's Valentine

Abra Staffin-Wiebe

Once upon a time, a slow, plodding sauropod fell in love with a beautiful dinosaur princess.

Although I didn't know it, the same day that my doctor told me I had six months left, my ex-wife learned she had a little short of nine months to go.

"That can't be right," I told my doctor. "We cured cancer. I splice genes—climate-adapted *dinosaur genes* —every day!"

"I'm sorry," he said. "This cancer is too aggressive for gene treatment. We can discuss palliative care, or trying to get you into an experimental study, but you need to prepare your loved ones for the worst. I can recommend a good end-of-life counselor ..."

I didn't really hear anything else he said. I nodded in the right places. I took the printouts he handed me. But there was a buzzing in my ears and a fog in my brain. The fog didn't lift until I was in the elevator and the doors opened to reveal Natalie.

Her father, the king of the dinosaurs, ate all her suitors after their gifts displeased her.

Natalie. My ex-wife. The mother of the only child I'd ever have, Daisy, a girl who would always be five years old and perfectly imperfect in our memories. Co-parent who covered for all my long hours in the lab. Partner in grief. Bitter enemy as we tore our marriage and each other apart with blame.

She glowed with happiness. The sign on the wall behind her said, "Reproductive Cloning."

For the rest of the elevator ride, the air was thick with all the words we didn't say.

The other suitors gave her meat. But the sauropod knew she loved flowers, so he set out on a quest to find the perfect blossom.

I called my lawyer.

"She can't do this!" I shouted. "The genes are half mine. She can't replace Daisy."

"There's no law preventing it. You could try a civil suit, but all she has to do is stall."

"Will you look into it? ...There's another issue, too." I told him about my diagnosis.

He agreed to meet me later that week. "I'll review your will. We can discuss its terms during our meeting," he said.

It was a long, lonely quest. The days grew short and long and short again before he discovered an amazing flower unlike anything he'd ever seen.

I told my manager my diagnosis.

"I'm so sorry," she said. "We'll do everything we can to help. I'll assign another engineer to the Theropod Project to shadow your role."

"Not necessary."

"The project completion timeline is eighteen months. Your diagnosis gives you six."

He knew the princess would love the flower, so he scooped the whole plant up carefully in his mouth and began the long trek home.

Natalie left me a message. "We have to talk," she said. "Please meet me for lunch." She named somewhere I'd never been, a place innocent of all associations.

I showed up, but I didn't order anything. "You're insane if you think I'll support this," I told her.

"I don't need your support," she said. "I'm doing this on my own. I only want a few pictures of you, so I can show my daughter where the other half of her genetic material comes from. Think about it." She paused. "I heard about your diagnosis. I'm sorry. For everything."

The sympathy in her voice drove me away faster than anger would have.

The blossom withered and went to seed along the way, but the plant still lived and so the sauropod persisted. With his every ponderous step, the plant shook like a dying bird.

Natalie was right; she didn't need my support. She would be a great single mother. She'd had plenty of practice solo parenting when we were married. The one thing that only I did, and she didn't, was read bedtime stories. Our daughter claimed Natalie read too fast and didn't do the voices right.

Daisy made me promise to always wake her up if she fell asleep before I got home.

So I always did.

I would wake Daisy up, give her a hug and a kiss, and then read the story. While her small, warm weight snuggled against my side, I told tales of princesses and pirates, dinosaurs and dragons, and fairies and unicorns. Often her eyelids fluttered shut again before I even finished a page, but I kept reading until she was deeply asleep.

When the sauropod returned, he found all the dinosaurs watching an asteroid plummeting toward the Earth. "You're too late," the dinosaur princess said. "But your gift is beautiful."

My will was simple. I didn't have many assets. I wouldn't be able to stay with the Theropod project until completion. By my contract, that meant I—or rather my heirs—wouldn't receive a split of the patent royalties.

After I was gone, what I left wouldn't make much difference. Not to my beneficiaries and not to the world.

My lawyer held out no hope for a lawsuit to stop Natalie.

When I persisted, he said, "I'm going to be blunt. We all die. Do you want your last act to be this bitter, losing battle? I've seen deaths that cause grief and deaths that cause rejoicing. The difference is in how we are remembered."

Daisy was gone, but I could still feel her warm, trusting weight. My love for her was a living thing. Could that legacy be passed down?

After I returned to work, I asked my manager, "What projects have shorter timelines?"

Everywhere that he had plodded, seeds had fallen and grown into a carpet of flowering plants. The princess leaned against him and together they admired the flowers.

By the time I finished the new project, even walking exhausted me. At the cancer's rate of growth, I had maybe one month left. My ex-wife had three months to go. She was round and radiant when she opened the door to me.

"I made videos of me reading bedtime stories, for our new daughter," I told her. I handed her a potted plant, elephantine and ancient and blooming for the first time in millennia. "And this. I named it Dinosaur's Valentine, after Daisy's favorite story."

"Love is never wasted," said the sauropod to his dinosaur princess. "Look at the beauty we created."

"The Dinosaur's Valentine" originally appeared in *Daily SF*
on 10 April 2020.

About the author

Abra Staffin-Wiebe loves optimistic science fiction, cheerful horror, and dark fantasy. Dozens of her short stories have appeared at publications including *Tor.com, F&SF, Escape Pod*, and *Odyssey Magazine*. She lives in Minneapolis, where she wrangles her children, pets, and the mad scientist she keeps in the attic. When not writing or wrangling, she collects folk tales and photographs — whatever stands still long enough to allow it. Discover more of her fiction at her website, www.aswiebe.com.

@cloudscudding

Copyright

Title information

Best Vegan SFF of 2020

ISBN: 978-1-64076-007-3 (e-book)
ISBN: 978-1-64076-008-0 (paperback)

Copyright

Works of fiction

All rights reserved

Moral rights asserted

Publisher

 plant based press

Plant Based Press is an imprint of
Metaphorosis Publishing
Neskowin, OR, USA

www.metaphorosis.com

"Metaphorosis" is a registered trademark.

Discounts available

Substantial discounts are available for educational institutions, including writing workshops. Discounts are also available for quantity purchases. For details, contact Metaphorosis at metaphorosis.com/about

Metaphorosis Publishing

Metaphorosis offers beautifully written science fiction and fantasy. Our imprints include:

Metaphorosis Magazine

plant based press

Metaphorosis Books

Driftwyrd

Vestige

Help keep Metaphorosis running at
Patreon.com/metaphorosis

See more about some of our books on the following pages.

Metaphorosis

a magazine of speculative fiction

Metaphorosis is an online speculative fiction magazine dedicated to quality writing. We publish an original story every week, along with author bios, interviews, and notes on story origins. Come and see us online at magazine.Metaphorosis.com

You can also find us at:
Twitter: @MetaphorosisMag, @MetaphorosisRev, @Metaphorosis
Facebook: www.facebook.com/metaphorosis

We publish monthly print and e-book issues, as well as yearly Best of and Complete anthologies.

Metaphorosis:
Best of 2020

The best science fiction and fantasy stories from *Metaphorosis* magazine's fifth year.

Metaphorosis 2020

All the stories from *Metaphorosis* magazine's fifth year. Fifty-two great SFF stories.

**Metaphorosis:
Best of 2019**

The best science fiction
and fantasy stories from
Metaphorosis magazine's
fourth year.

Metaphorosis 2019

All the stories from
Metaphorosis magazine's
fourth year. Fifty-two great
SFF stories.

**Metaphorosis:
Best of 2018**

The best science fiction
and fantasy stories from
Metaphorosis magazine's
third year.

Metaphorosis 2018

All the stories from
Metaphorosis magazine's
third year. Fifty-two great
SFF stories.

Metaphorosis: Best of 2017

The best science fiction and fantasy stories from *Metaphorosis* magazine's *second* year.

Metaphorosis 2017

All the stories from *Metaphorosis* magazine's second year. Fifty-three great SFF stories.

Metaphorosis: Best of 2016

The best science fiction and fantasy stories from *Metaphorosis* magazine's first year.

Metaphorosis 2016

Almost all the stories from *Metaphorosis* magazine's first year.

Plant Based Press

Vegan-friendly science fiction and fantasy, including an annual anthology of the year's best SFF stories.

Best Vegan SFF of 2020

The best vegan-friendly science fiction and fantasy stories of 2020!

Best Vegan SFF of 2019

The best vegan-friendly science fiction and fantasy stories of 2019!

Best Vegan SFF of 2018

The best vegan-friendly science fiction and fantasy stories of 2018!

Best Vegan SFF of 2017

The best vegan-friendly science fiction and fantasy stories of 2017!

Best Vegan SFF of 2016

The best vegan-friendly science fiction and fantasy stories of 2016!

 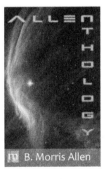

Susurrus

A darkly romantic story of magic, love, and suffering.

Allenthology: Volume I

A quarter century of SFF, including the full contents of the collections *Tocsin, Start with Stones,* and *Metaphorosis.*

Verdage

Science fiction and fantasy books for writers – full of great stories, but with an additional focus on the craft of speculative fiction writing.

Reading 5X5 x2

Duets

How do authors' voices change when they collaborate?

A round-robin of five talented science fiction and fantasy authors collaborating with each other and writing solo.

Including stories by Evan Marcroft, David Gallay, J. Tynan Burke, L'Erin Ogle, and Douglas Anstruther.

Score

an SFF symphony

What if stories were written like music? *Score* is an anthology of varied stories arranged to follow an emotional score from the heights of joy to the depths of despair – but always with a little hope shining through.

Reading 5X5

Five stories, five times

Twenty-five SFF authors, five base stories, five versions of each – see how different writers take on the same material, with stories in contemporary and high fantasy, soft and hard SF, and a mysterious 'other' category.

Reading 5X5

Writers' Edition

All the stories from the regular, readers' edition, plus two extra stories, the story seed, and authors' notes on writing. Over 100 pages of additional material specifically aimed at writers.

Vestige

Novelettes, novellas, and novels by Metaphorosis authors.

Tower of Mud and Straw

Yaroslav Barsukov

2021 Nebula finalist
for best novella!

The Queen ruined his life. He would do anything to reclaim it... or so he thought.

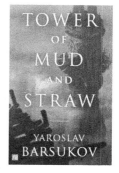

Made in the USA
Monee, IL
24 July 2021